Book Two The Courthouse Series

RUTTER INDUSTRIES

by

Carolyn Marks Johnson

Production Manager: Kimberly Verhines

ISBN: 978-1-62288-262-5

For more information:
Stephen F. Austin State University Press
P.O. Box 13007 SFA Station
Nacogdoches, Texas 75962
sfapress@sfasu.edu
936-468-1078

Distributed by the Texas A&M University Press Book Consortium
www.tamupress.com

CONFIDENTIAL COMMUNICATIONS

CONFIDENTIAL: Entrusted with the confidence of another or with his secret affairs or purposes; intended to be held in confidence or kept secret; done in confidence.

CONFIDENTIAL COMMUNICATIONS: Privileged comunications such as those between spouses, attorney-client, confessor-penitent, etc. Such are privileged at the option of the spouse-witness, client-witness, and penitent-witness. A Confidential Communication is a statement (or letter or tape) made under circumstances showing that the speaker intended only for ears of the person addressed; thus if communication is made in presence of a third party whose presence is not reasonably necessary for the communication, it is not privileged.

There are certain classes of communications, passing between persons who stand in a confidential or fiduciary relation to each other (or who, on account of their relation to each other (or who, on account of their relative situation, are under a duty of secrecy and fidelity), which the law will not permit to be divulged or allow them to be inquired into in a court of justice, for the sake of public policy and the good order of society.

PRIVILEGED COMMUNICATIONS: Those statements made by certain persons within a protected relationship such as husband-wife, attorney-client, priest-penitent, and the like, which the law protects from forced disclosure on the witness stand at the option of the witness client, penitent, spouse. The extent of the privilege is governed by State Statutes.[1]

---

1   Henry Campbell Black, *Black's Law Dictionary Definitions of the Terms and Phrases of American and English Jurisprudence Ancient and Modern*, 5th Ed., West Publishing, St. Paul, Minn. 1979

CONTENTS

My son, Jacob Dwight Johnson, tells the men who are attracted to my daughters and granddaughters to be prepared because they each are high maintenance women. He knows that his father prepared them for that life. My husband, Jake, loved having five daughters and persuaded each of them, in turn, that it only costs a nickel more to insist on first class! Jake AND I also loved our son Dwight, and JAKE taught him to fly by the age of twelve and helped him buy an airplane by sixteen! I would say that is pretty high maintenance too!

THAT OLD MARINE CORPS FIGHTER PILOT HAS ALWAYS BEEN OUR HERO, FOR MY CHILDREN AND ME, AND HE ALWAYS WILL BE. HE LOVES THIS SERIES BECAUSE HE KNOWS THE GOOD PARTS CAME FROM HIM!

CHAPTER ONE
Fee Lo Gets a Job

"Shar-r-r-r-on," he says, letting the r roll off his tongue. "You don't look like a Shar-r-r-r-on."

"No? What does a Sharon look like?"

"You know. Somebody dangerous. Like Sharon Stone in that movie."

She laughs good naturedly.

"Well I am a Sharon and proud to be one. My Mother is also a Sharon. You know, Rose of Sharon, that's her name. Rose Sharon and I'm the opposite Sharon Rose. She never liked the order of her name."

"Well I like it," Fee Lo decides and reaches a hand in her direction, which she takes and shakes smoothly and firmly.

"Good grip," he says. "You must have played softball as a girl."

"Pitcher," she confirms. "Went to State. Came in second."

"Well that ain't right," Fee Lo says.

"Sure wasn't," Sharon Donaldson agrees. "It still burns."

"What's a nice girl like you, doing …".

"Don't say it," she interrupts. "It's beneath you and you're doing well in this interview. What kind of job are you looking for?"

"Anything," he answers. "Looks like my time to go Rutter has come and here I am. I'm a legacy if that makes a difference. My Dad was Rutter in the Valley. Mama retired five years ago. Also in the Valley."

"Well, that's two good recommendations," she says. "You come from solid Rutter stock. Your tests are all good. The psyches show a little pent-up anger; but considering what you do…."

"Did," he says. "No more. That's over. I'm going corporate."

"Did, I should have said. I knew about all that. Read it in the paper. You won though, didn't you? I saw the hero spread!"

"It got covered on a slow day. How did you know?"

"Oh, we have our ways. We make it our business to know what

goes on in our community. That's why we always come out on top as well. We do our homework."

"I can only imagine," he says, although he not only can imagine, he knows it to be true. Rutter has a bigger security staff than many cities and all airports.

She smiles at this as if she sees through the lie and goes on: "You should have no difficulty here; but given your special qualifications, you might be more interested in our security force than the one you worked for before. We pay a lot more than they do."

"That ain't hard to do, Miss Shar-r-r-on Donaldson. You got time for coffee?"

"I think I can," Miss Donaldson says with a smile. "We'll take this chance for me to show you around, introduce you to a few people, who need to say yes. And then, yes, I'll take you up on that cup of coffee."

CHAPTER TWO
The Courthouse Run

I do my usual courthouse run with Phyllis leading me case to case.

I am Alexandra McLeod, known as Shadow by anybody who knew me growing up, because I was always underfoot.

Phyll hands me a stack of files.

"These are ready for you," she says. "I read the papers with them as usual, but on these," she says, isolating five files. "You are going to do them alone and you'll have to go over the plea. I will do these and have them ready in Judge Tamara's Court when you get there."

The ones I handle alone are few and far between. Part of the reason is that my associate, Phyllis MacArthur—just like the general she has to be related to—takes a personal interest in those who come from her church. They will get her special treatment, usually a support group, NA and AA attendance, if drugs or alcohol-related, and transportation to and from reporting. Irrespective, I have to be the last one touching the file and supporting the plea at the bench. As she reminds me, we do not forget who the lawyer is.

I note the majority of even more have been initialed by the client, meaning she has read and explained it to them. When she does leave one for me, she doesn't do it without telling me what I should be able to do on the file.

Whether English or Spanish, she is fluent. The only second language coming from me is a New York accent when I forget.

Most plea work in the criminal courts has become rote because there is so much of it, and two-thirds of that is possession in varying amounts, and it's a never-ending process.

Use.

Plea.

Go to jail.

Get out.

Use again.

Plea.

Go to Jail and on and on.

"Eddie Stephens wants this one to plead more than we do," she tells me, knowing I will understand that she wants me to sweeten the deal.

"The client likes the deal?" I ask her. She just gives me that look. When I think the client should not take it, I tell them and tell them what the options are. Most of the prosecutors I routinely deal with are reasonable and will shave off a little time from the sentence or even offer probation to the eligible.

A lot of people, including the DA's assistants, don't like probation and think it's a free ride. Probation, along with deferred, is actually one of the few win-wins at the Courthouse. The Defendant pays for both and if still eligible for Deferred, can enter a plea, do the work, pay the fees and at some point, if he or she keeps out of trouble for the duration of the Deferred, the DA will recommend, and the Judge will sign a dismissal of the charge on the state's motion or at least grant a Petition for Non-Disclosure of the Record.

If an accused is not deferred-eligible due to prior convictions, Probation is the next best thing. They do the same, stay out of trouble, pay the fees, do the rehabilitation training and show successful completion on their record but they have to enter a plea of guilty, which sticks, meaning it stays on their record.

Deferred is preferred but both processes give them a second chance to reestablish themselves in the community. Besides that, it saves the taxpayer money. I think that's important. It costs more than $60.00 to house an inmate one day; it costs them $6.00 generally to be on alternative sentencing.

Probation and Deferred are second chances to those who just frankly mess up in a weak moment, which is what happened here in my opinion. And my guy is seventeen, so he just got recognized by the State of Texas as an adult.

And, those of us who give a damn, as Fee Lo says, believe rehabilitation is a benefit to society. And we see that, frankly with probation and deferred.

I make it through the set of cases Phyll gave me and those in

Judge Tamara's Court. We meet in the Hallway and start back to the last setting.

After the third person asks me how Fee Lo is doing, I answer that he's doing great, look at Phyllis, and stand my ground while I call and make an appointment with Sharon Donaldson at Rutter.

"You know he's probably just met another woman," Phyllis warns me.

"Something's not right; I know he was at Rutter."

"How? You can't rely on it just because he said it is so."

"No," I tell her.

"Well, what do you know that I don't?"

"I'll tell you later. Is this the last case of the morning?"

"Yeah, I saved it for you. Edward Stevens asked me to."

"Because?"

"I don't know, he just said to tell you to come see him."

"Okay, I'll do it. You want to go to Rutter with me?"

"I can, but I'll need to leave now because we have two kids coming by that Judge Tamara appointed us on."

"Okay you meet with them. I'll go see His Highness."

Eddie Stevens got back to his office just as I got there and he drops a big stack of files on his desk and loosens his tie.

"I can come back later," I offer. "If you need to change, that is?"

"No, no," he says and blushes, but finishes removing his tie and throws it on the desk. "I hate those things. I want to ask you about something. Have a seat," he offers.

I prop on the edge of the straight-backed chair he put by his desk for lawyers. The message does not go over my head—don't get comfortable is what that chair says—so I sit as close as I can manage to the edge so he'll know I am not eager to hang around either. It forces my back into an even straighter line. Two can play that game anyway, and it's not my nature to throw a fight.

"Well, it seems I've mislaid the file. Got time for lunch?"

"Not today," I say. "I have a couple things I need to do. You could help me with something."

"Sure, shoot."

"Tell me what you know about Rutter Industries."

"Well, what I know about Rutter Industries would keep us here the rest of the day."

"Well, how about the short version?"

"Oldest modern company on the island. Biggest taxpayer. Biggest staff. Biggest chunk of the world's business but for Atlas and Exxon Corp. Energy. Oil. Petroleum byproducts. Plastics. Construction, here and abroad. Finance. The works. That's it in a nutshell."

"You didn't say political powerhouse."

"Oh that, too, for sure," he says. "And in trouble with the law more than once; but always emerges paying a large fine and smelling like a patriotic rose. Why do you need to know?" he asks, moving a file from the top and sliding it underneath the stack.

"I can tell you're busy," I say. "I won't keep you any longer."

I seize my chance and leave, not ready to have this man think I am an alarmist, but I am not able to do lunch with anyone at the Courthouse either because I like to keep my relationships and work separate.

I can't eat anyway. I sense danger and when that happens, my stomach ties itself up into little knots and refuses food.

CHAPTER THREE
Introduction to Rutter

I pull up at Rutter on the Harley. No chance of being incognito on that noise-production machine, but it occurs to me that if Fee Lo is around, he'll recognize the sound and know I'm there. Perhaps he'll at least be curious enough to want to know what I'm up to and call me later tonight.

Sharon Donaldson greets me politely, but woman to woman here, I can tell something is wrong.

She hits a pencil on the desk and seems pre-occupied.

"Would you like to go for a walk and get a cup of coffee?" she asks with a laugh, "I haven't had mine this morning, and I guess I didn't realize how addicted I've grown to caffeine."

"I understand," I confess. "I live on the stuff myself. A coffeemaker is my only appliance. As long as I have that, I can do anything. Why not? Let's go have a cup of coffee."

"That's the Southern thing, you understand," she says, taking her change purse from her purse and putting it in her lower desk drawer."

Her phone rings.

"Oh my," she says in response. "I didn't realize that."

She looks at me apologetically.

"I have somebody else here. Looks like I get no coffee after all." She shoves her coin purse into her bag and closes the drawer. "What was it exactly that you needed from me?"

"I need to talk to you about my friend, Felipe Hernandez."

She looks confused. Shakes her head a couple of times.

"I wish I could help. But I don't know such a person."

"You must," I insist. "He told me he met you. He said you were the most interesting woman he'd met in a long time." Sharon Donaldson blushes easily. As I suspected, Fee Lo would have found a way to make a good impression on this attractive woman, who looks as straight arrow as could be in her conservative gray skirt and white blouse and pearls.

"He said he had more fun with you over coffee than any date he'd had in months, although he knew that was not a date. He said you talked about your softball career. Going to State. Coming in second. Called it a crime against women because you should have won."

"Well, all of those things must be true then."

"That's what I was hoping."

"But he must have met with someone else, who impressed him that much."

"Sharon, you can talk to me. Did he give you the rush?"

I see a tear forming in her left eye, which she dabs with a Kleenex she takes from her desk. "I told you I never met him. I can't help you. You have to go. I have a real appointment. I wish I could give you more time and the help that you need. I just don't have either."

She practically pushes me to the door.

I know then I should have just refused to leave.

But that did not seem to be an option.

Her assistant keeps her head down until I am out of the room. I look back long enough to see her duck it quickly again when she sees me looking back into the glass-walled office. With a helper that timid there is certainly no reason for Sharon Donaldson to lock her door as soon as I leave. I hear a man's voice in a hushed whisper and want to stand by the door and try to listen, but I actually feel danger. She is either a colossal liar or somebody at Rutter Industries is calling strange shots! I am certain Sharon Donaldson's assistant pushed me from the office and locked the door.

I go back.

"I have one other person to see," I tell her. "Is Jack McNelly's office close to here?"

The timid assistant shakes her head from side to side quickly.

"Mr. McNelly does not take callers," she whispers.

"He promised to see me," I lie. "I think he and I may have gone to school together."

"He's not from around here," she says, struggling to be polite and obviously one hundred percent certain I am laying down a trail of lies, which I am.

"Neither am I," I say. "I remember him from DC, actually," I hand her my card and ask him to call.

I leave, ironically on Fee Lo's Harley, unable to disguise my exit or turn around and sneak back in and talk to others. I also didn't have the nerve.

CHAPTER FOUR
The Morgue

After my pleas I go to the *Enterprise*, which is directly across the street from the Courthouse, and head for the Morgue. In a newspaper, the morgue is a place where stories go to be buried for all time; forgotten but preserved forever. I did filing in a newspaper's morgue during college and became fascinated with the vast amount of often overlooked primary evidence around and I know how to do what I am asking to do.

The quality of newspaper morgues varies greatly. This one is good. It has an attitude through its chief librarian, Susan Miller, who seems to be a no-nonsense woman and who is not only efficient but in control of her environment. I learn that the *Enterprise's* Morgue is the oldest in Texas and that it has original documents and microfiche copies of every newspaper it ever published as well as filmed copies of newer issues and then computer preservation of recent editions.

"It's good to see you. I wondered when you would be back," Susan Miller says. "How did the Hurley Brown matter go?"

"Oh it turned out fine." I tell her but say nothing more because the rumor has him framing charges for kids and assisting Henry Ace Tuttle, who tried to kill Judge Judd Baker. I'm beginning to think Tuttle is his runner for clients and goods, meaning whatever contraband, i. e. drugs, that come his way.

The Morgue has letters written to the paper by Texas heroes such as Stephen F. Austin, Sam Houston, and others. It is a jewel of a room and reeks of historical importance, no doubt enhanced by Ms. Miller's attitude.

Short, 5 foot, 3 inches, brown hair styled in a nice straight but turned under at the tips pageboy style, she has clear skin, nice hazel eyes and a direct manner. I like her and she told me my first time here that we have a friend in common, my legal assistant, who calls herself my kick-ass sidekick. Phyllis is Miss Miller's Sunday School teacher.

I ask for any file that she might have on Lorena Burnett, also known as Babe.

"That may be confidential," she reminds me.

"I thought you might have a profile page," I say. "Surely an article was done about her when she got the Headliner's Award."

"Well, we can certainly check," she says and leads me back into a room containing row after row of tall books containing copies of the *Enterprise* that were not thrown away when put on tape, because "that would have been a travesty and counter to good history practices," Susan Miller says.

Along one edge, small tables bearing reading machines line the back wall and file cabinets stretch to cover both sides of the room. She leads me to one marked B and opens the drawer, goes through every file herself and pulls one out.

"You've got a good nose for this," she says and leads me to a library table surrounded by six pristine light oak chairs. She spreads open the file and gives me instructions about touching the documents carefully and tells me that if I find what I am looking for, it may be easier to note the date of publication and read it from the machine. I shake my head in agreement.

She leaves me and returns to her desk because another person has come. I hear murmurs but no real conversation until I am soon joined by Phyllis MacArthur, who takes a seat across the table, and smiles.

"You followed me," I say.

"Great minds," she says. "Remember I'm the one who had to listen to your Boy Wonder blow smoke about her and how she thinks."

"Fair enough," I say.

"I want to help," she adds. "I feel this isn't right too. Something is going on."

I share a stack of clippings that is a mixture. One category, actual clippings of her stories, the other, articles about her. I find what I am looking for and pull it out to note the date and read it. I intend to ask for a copy as soon as I go through them all.

"Babe got a state Headliner's Award for her murder story," Phyll says as she starts through her stack. "That's impressive."

"Maybe that's why her goal is now a Pulitzer."

"It would be mine, if I could write a sentence," Phyll says as she continues to thumb through the significant stack of documents. Meanwhile, Susan Miller is now hovering to meet Phyll's needs and takes off with our first stack of documents to make copies for us. She also pulls the reels if we want to view them on the reader. I do so for the profile after the Headliners.

As I read it I wonder how much of this is accurate and how much is Babe's backstory for Babe, but I take notes on the significant things that I need.

CHAPTER FIVE
Looking for Babe

The woman on the phone has a voice that is clearly East Texas or parts south. She coughs and it frankly sounds to me like she spits into something before answering. I picture something unpleasant, such as snuff or a wad of tobacco stuffed in the cheeks; but the voice is nice when she recovers and returns to the phone.

"Excuse me," she says. "I'm having trouble with my lungs and tend to lose my voice when I least expect it."

"I am so sorry to hear that," I say. "Do they know what's causing it?"

"Probably my old man's cigarettes. Smoked Camels. Blew them toward me by long habit.

"I'm looking for Lavern Burnett," I tell her.

"That's me," she says. "Is something wrong?"

"No I say. I'm actually looking for "Babe" Burnett, I thought Lavern might be her given name."

"That's my name," she says and coughs again and spits. I wait. "She ain't been here in a long time."

"Can we talk about that?"

"I don't know nuthin' to tell you."

"Are you her Mother?"

"Yes, Ma'am."

"When did you last see her or talk to her?"

"It wuz probably six years, I'd say. Who are you anyway?"

"I should have told you that first off. My name is Alexandra McLeod and I am a personal friend, who needs to find her."

"She done somethin' to be in trouble?"

"Not that I know about," I say. "Does the name Felipe Hernandez mean anything to you?"

"A Mexican?" she asks. "Can't say that it does. Are you part of that man who called my house last week about this same time?"

"Did he give you his name?"

"Naw, just said he was the law. Didn't even tell me from where."

"Can I come visit you? You're not actually that far away from me," I say, somewhat surprised to discover that Babe never got far from her origins if this is it.

"Ain't gonna cost me nothin' to talk is it?"

She cackles a little bit and I laugh.

Phyll and I shut things down and drive to Kilgore. It fills the afternoon but we still have light with which to find the location, a petite, unpainted frame cottage that has air dried gray as it aged and that is surrounded by tall Texas pines that are green and give off a freshness in the late afternoon breeze.

The woman I think is Babe's Mama sits on the porch and looks as if she has been sitting there waiting for us since we called. The glider slides; it has seen better days but still works. In one hand, she is holding a large plastic cup into which she regularly spits and has a glass of tea with melted ice, which balances beside her on the glider. Mosquitos are already coming out and she and I slap at one at the same time. Phyll seems immune, but she surprises me by saying:

"Sister Lavern, how are you today?"

"Lord knows I've had better days, Honey," she says.

"I'll bet we passed your church on the way out here."

The woman smiles.

A ghost of Babe hovers over her face but this beauty has faded and settled in for the countdown. I thought maybe what I heard was snuff spitting, an old Texas habit, but it wasn't: Laverne has some type of lung disease.

We take a seat on metal porch seats that also have seen better days but they still rock back and forth slightly and Phyll and I immediately set off the same rhythm as Babe's Mother.

"Can I get you some tea?" she asks.

"We stopped at Dairy Queen about twenty miles back and I admit to being pretty much saturated with iced tea."

"Know what you mean," she says. "It's hot out here and not much better inside. If we're gonna talk about Babe, we better do it. I get to bed pretty early now."

She continues to glide. Phyll rocks. And I lean forward. The three rhythms set off a symphony of creaks and groans.

"Can you just talk to me about Babe? Was she born here?"

"Not in this house, I had to go to the regional hospital 'cause I was already having lung trouble by then, but we didn't talk about it none. Doctor said she was too little and might need incubation. She wuz right. I came home before Babe by about twelve weeks. It wuz almost like Babe already knew enough about this place to already know she never wanted to come here."

"But she did?"

"Oh, yes, she did all right. She grew up pretty fast out here. Her Daddy stopped smoking in the house when the doctor said it wuz killin' me, and she wouldn't let the baby come home at all if he didn't take it outside."

"And he did?"

"Oh, he did, all right. Took it so far outside he ran a cord to the barn and did his radio listening and then television out there so he could keep smoking."

"Is he still here?"

"Naw, he died. The next one left right after he ran her off."

"Do you mind sharing that? How old was she?

"Fourteen," Lavern says, "Said she was tired of him telling her what to do the way he did. He was very firm with her. That day, she actually climbed that tree, right over there, the tall chinaberry tree. That branch wasn't as high then. Sat right there a good twelve hours with him yellin' up the tree, 'Come on down now, you got to take your licking and we'll be over it.'"

She resettles herself in the glider and takes a sip of tea.

"He paced; she sat right there not moving from that tree branch. Then he got tired, I guess and got in the truck and took off. After a while she came down.

"Mama I can't take it anymore," she told me and I watched her pack up her things in one of them grocery carry bags with the straps. She was so little it fit on her shoulder. Didn't have much in it. By then there was nothing she wanted from here. Even me.

"Mama," she told me. "I know you can't help it and he's all you got; but I can't sit still for this no more. It hurts when he works off his drunks on me and it makes me feel worthless."

"Did you tell anyone?"

"Of course not, Mama; I know how things work. You need him at the lumber yard and not in jail."

"'I thank you for that Lorena,' I told her and I watched her walk down that dusty path right there. Crossing the field. It hurt so bad in my heart 'cause I didn't feel I could do anything different.

"But she was born wanting away from this place. Like she didn't belong here and knew it even when she was a baby.

"There was a boy on the other side of the fields and I knew his folks would take her in. She thought she was in love with him. He wanted to be a traveling preacher and Lorena had a pretty good voice. I never heard nothing for about six years. She was old enough by then to be out of high school and working. I know she was because she started sending the money orders in my name only so he couldn't cash them.

"When I could get somebody from the Church to take me there, I'd go into town and cash 'em in. Sometimes he tried to take the money, but he knew I wuz sick even then and she said do what the doctor told me.

"Did she ever send you addresses or information about other places where she had been?"

"No, just the money. A lot of it came from Tyler for awhile, and I think that's where the boy was preachin.' I don't know if they ever married, but a woman at the church said they were living together and doing traveling revivals. She could've done that."

"Then she started sending regular bank checks out of Galveston and that's the last I heard."

"When was the last check?"

"Bout three months ago. You asked a lot of questions," she says, "and I answered them 'cause you seem to think she's in trouble. Is she?"

"I'm not really sure," I tell this poor lonely soul. "I am looking for her for a friend I think might be with her. But also for us. We need to help her if she is in trouble."

"I don't reckon you'll come back here to tell me. She sent me this cell phone once, but I never figured out how to use it."

"Do you have it?" I ask.

"Probably in there somewhere," she said.

She thinks the cell phone is still in the box, she says. I ask Phyll, who is experienced manipulating cellphones, if she can get it running. We follow Lavern Burnett into her small cottage and discover it is one big room with a kitchen in one corner and a bathroom in the other marked off by cloth panels suspended from the ceiling and an oil heater in the very center. Across the front, the single room serves as living and sleeping space. She rummages for a while in one drawer then slaps her head with both hands.

"Now I remember!" She pulls a box from beneath the couch and hands it to Phyllis, who takes out the cell phone, finds the support items beneath the phone and plugs it in.

"How long have you had it?" Phyllis asks.

"'Bout a year, I think," Lavern answers.

After it charges for a while, Phyll finds a low signal and walks out into the front yard where she manages to get two bars but is unable to get into the phone.

"Did she give you a password, Sister?" Phyll asks.

"Naw, I don't think so. She said all I had to do was type 'Babe' into the phone and the phone opens.

Phyll shows her how to get into the phone and how to type Babe into it, but the woman lays it on her lap without trying.

"Did she say anything when she sent the phone?" Phyll asks.

"Just that I should type in 'babe' if I wanted to talk to her."

"Did you try that?"

"Naw, I thought it was too late; and I was always afraid that she was gonna say something that would send the law out. Till he finally wandered off too. Made me feel bad about how things were actually. Sometimes it's better not to know."

"And she never called?"

"Not that I know about."

"Is there anyone we could talk to that might be able to give us some clue about finding her? What about your husband? Her step-father. Do we know where he is?"

"Wouldn't matter," she says. "Won't her daddy anyway."

"What happened to her Daddy?"

"He died. He was cutting down timber and a tree fell on him. That's how we met my husband. At her Daddy's funeral."

"And the boy?"

"Well." She sits quietly for a while. "Don't recollect his name after all this time; but the preacher knows that young man and whether or not she went with him."

I ask for photographs and she gives us a couple of faded prints in black and white. One is a pretty child with short curly hair, wearing a dress with a single ruffle around the bottom and a sash that ties in the back. The bow is so large it stands out from her waist like wings. She is smiling and holding a small puppy. The other is an older child, but still a child, probably 12 or 13 with a developing body wearing jeans and a t-shirt. The dog stands beside her.

"What's its name?" I ask Lavern.

"I have to think," Lavern says. "It's two different dogs actually. Both were named Roger and that's the boy's name. Roger. Roger something, my brain just won't work now that I am on so much medicine."

"You said a lawman called you or came by last week. Can you tell me anything more about him?"

"No, he never came by, and I never talked to him. Always been afraid of the law. They don't do you no good, you know that don't you?"

"Sure," I say to be agreeable. As a general rule I like lawmen and trust them for the most part. And most are good, hard-working people.

"I didn't like the way he talked. He had a rough, mean voice. I told him I didn't know who he's talking about and he must have the wrong number. I could tell he didn't like it cause he slammed down the phone right in my face."

CHAPTER SIX
A Place Can Have Character

Phyll and I back slowly out of Lavern's yard to avoid stirring up dust. I feel guilty because it's virtually impossible. Most of East Texas seems to be fine grain sand covered by long and short leafed pines that grow taller than any trees I've seen East of the Mississippi. I love the fact they drop their pine needles into what seems to be a smooth brown blanket on the ground.

Way out West, I know the trees are a thousand years older and dominate wherever they get space and these East Texas Pines cannot compete with the silent majesty of Red Woods and Sequoias. It's hard to imagine, but at one time, I've read, this entire area of earth was a land for virgin trees.

And in a time when wood was the way everything grew into being, from trains to ships that sailed still uncharted waters, that kind of wood drew adventurers because wood meant wealth. Every major power had its uncut forests on which to feast and which provided an economic basis for their worth, in part.

When we get to the strip of sand that leads to the highway, Phyll stops and we look around. The Lumber Company hasn't gotten here yet, but it's easy to see why Lavern stays put in her tiny cottage that looks too small for a comfortable existence.

"These trees are beautiful," I say. We are completely surrounded and seem to be miniatures in a different world.

"It's a different world out here for sure," Phyll says, reading my mind.

"We never see anything like this where we are."

"No, they all went into houses and roads. Wherever people are, the world becomes less magical."

"That was a sweet lady," I say, testing Phyll's reaction.

"She let her daughter fend for herself. Don't know that I could have done that." The activist in Phyll is surfacing; but the goodness in her heart for all lies just beneath that, holding her back until she gets a cause. Apparently, Lavern did just that. "Let her daughter be the victim of a man, who wasn't even her real father!"

While Phyll's primary commitment often seems to favor males, which she believes are the weaker link in the species, she has a special place in her heart, I think, for put-upon-women. Lavern must have opened up that vein because Phyll has flashed more anger in the way she stopped breathing than I've seen in a long time.

"You can see right off the bat why Babe is Babe," she tells me, somewhat as if it might be my fault she had questions about Babe, as did I.

"An abused child never grows out of it," she says.

"I know that Phyll. Why do you think I do what I do? You're not the only one who trusts that she's acting in faith for the best result for these people we work for. I couldn't stay here if I didn't think that what I was doing makes a difference for them."

"I knew there was something behind it all," Phyll says, returning to Babe. "And I know there's something behind you, little girl, that brings you here to this unlettered paradise when you could be out front and center anywhere you chose."

We have reached the highway and stopping lets me take a deep, long breath.

"That was taxing. More than I thought a thing could be," I say. "And I do care about, Little Babe, as Fee Lo would say. Now we both know why. She never got a break."

"Except she looks like a million dollars," Phyll says.

"And we come on like some of our $20.-a-night-neighbors."

We don't laugh.

It's not funny.

"This place has character," I say but Phyll looks at me with squinty little eyes.

"But you learned nothing if you didn't get the hint, the flaws in the character when they are here can run deep all over this area."

CHAPTER SEVEN
Called by God

Phyllis lets out a long sigh and then breathes in deeply.

"Wow!" she says.

"Are you game for the preacher?" I ask.

"We passed the Church on the main highway," she says in confirmation. "It's actually First Church of the One True God. I don't know that Church."

"You know anything about what they do?"

"Nope. But out here they could be snake handlers for all I know. I wouldn't be surprised after all that we just heard."

We drive along in silence until we get to the farm to market road, which is a step up from the trail we have been on but still not as good as the state highway we came in on. Due to its size, Texas has a somewhat complicated road system that follows its progress and goes from dirt trails to farm to market roads to highways—county, state, and interstate.

We do not have far to go. The church is on the right. It looks to be about 20 by 30 feet with a peaked roof and a small cupola for a steeple. A dirt track circles it; and you can see where a generation of cars have made their mark on the surroundings. The path leads to the back, and we drive in that direction until it becomes obvious that we are at the entrance to the parsonage, a neat double-wide trailer running a greater length than the church itself.

A single light glows at one end outside and a flicker within the open front door proves to be the blue light of a television. Three steps have been extended to form a small porch with a make-do rail of used fence posts. It looks clean and well kept.

I knock and when a middle-aged man with balding hair comes to the door, Phyll takes over.

"Pastor, we are looking for information about one of your Sisters in Christ."

I couldn't keep a straight face if I tried that approach; but for Phyllis it is as natural and sincere as she can be and as serious as a heart attack.

"Come in Sisters," he says. "I'm Preacher Shutte."

Phyll defers to me. "Reverend Shutte," I say. "We just visited with your parishioner Lavern Burnett and she said you might be able to tell us a little bit about a boy named Roger and Mrs. Burnett's daughter, Lorena Burnett."

He looks at us, long and hard. "And who are you?"

"Forgive me, I should have told you immediately. I am Alexandra McLeod and this is my associate Miss Phyllis MacArthur. We are trying to locate Lorena Burnett, also known as "Babe" by her Mother. Can you help us?"

"Well she's right about my helping, but I have to think about it, 'cause some of what I'd have to say would not be Christian of me." He is actually watching a popular gospel music program on his television and has his Bible open on his chair's arm. He starts to turn it down, and Phyll says: "Oh, let that play out. I love that song."

"I love that quartet," he says. "Watch 'em every week."

"I do when I can," Phyll says. "We don't want you to break your witness, Pastor," Phyllis says, cutting in. "But it is very important that we get as much information as possible because this woman may be in great danger."

"She's already sacrificed her soul," he says. "I'd be surprised if her soul isn't too far damned already."

We both sit back in total surprise, which is not feigned. Men don't usually talk about Babe with that kind of negative vehemence.

"What did she do, Pastor?" Phyll's voice is full of sympathy and empathy for this man and it is genuine Phyllis. We can see the burden he bears on his face. Deep furrows line his forehead. He looks up with a painful grimace, and Phyll knows exactly how to answer. This is her jurisdiction.

"You must follow what God wants you to do and only you can know that."

He gives her a studied look.

"That boy you are looking for is my son, Roger Shutte," the pastor says and tears fill his eyes and drip over onto his hollow cheeks. "Was, I should say," he continues. "Was until that girl came into his life and changed its direction."

"I'm very sorry," Phyll and I say in unison. This is a man who appears to be losing his reason to live.

"The way I feel about her is coming near to defeating my life with Christ. I got the call forty years ago in those woods right behind this house and this House of God. I had gone into the woods to pray. Something was calling me strong and as I walked among these tall Texas pines, the sky opened where an old tree had fallen and I sank onto that log and felt the power of the Lord sweep all over me. I looked up and the sun came out from the clouds and I could hear angels singing. I knew what I had to do. I told the Lord to guide me and I would follow. And I saw the face of God in those clouds. I built this Church on the very spot that happened at and by my own hand with Roger's help and he was as strong a witness as I have tried to be. The Lord sent people to worship and I've never left this spot.

"We took that girl in, my wife and I. I knew what had happened to that girl was wrong and that she was damaged goods; Devil was already in her. I had the warning. But my boy would see none of that; she drug my boy right down with her. He died to Christ. He died to me. I'm sure he died to her as soon as she found something better."

"I'm so sorry," again, we spoke in unison.

"Thank you. It helps to know that."

"Do you think he would talk to us?" Phyll says this quietly. The old man grows real quiet and seems to think things over.

"If you promise to tell him the truth about her, I will tell you how to find him. If you're not gonna do that, I just want you to leave him alone. He has a life now. He just doesn't walk with God anymore."

"Do you know when they left you?"

He turns to a middle page in his Bible, pulls out a thin sheet of notepaper and reads the date from that page.

"That's when my life became the test of Job," he says. "I brought Jezebel into my world, wanting to do right; but knowing women, who claim such abuse are suffering God's will. She destroyed my family."

We said goodbye to Pastor Shutte.

He did not give us a picture of Roger but he did allow me to copy three of them on my cellphone. One when the boy was about fifteen, standing with Babe who had a large "X" drawn over her picture. One was when he graduated with a Master of Business Administration from Southern Methodist University, a real surprise, and one was with his wife and three stair-stepped children who appeared to be two boys of nearly the same age and a girl, who was somewhat younger.

"What time are we due in Court tomorrow?" I ask Phyll as we are settling back into the car.

She had asked Preacher Shutte to say a prayer for both of us and had written out and handed him a contribution to his congregation.

"I am going to suggest that we drive as far as Tyler and go into Dallas and see Roger Shutte as early as we catch him at work and then head back for the docket.

"We would be real late," Phyll says.

"Denise will hold it if we are late, won't she, or roll us over?"

"I don't have the file," she says, and adds "But it's a case I'm worried about."

"Okay, we go back. I'll call him during the day and see if he'll talk. I haven't been to Big D in a while."

"He may not talk to you, if he knows what it's about," she warns.

"I'll think of something. Did you see what that kid's name is?"

She looks through my pictures. Scribbled on the back of the copy of the family are the names in order: "Roger, Sandy, John, Jack and Babe."

"Well, I'll be damned."

"Yes, I thought so too. He probably needs to talk."

CHAPTER EIGHT
From Tent to Tower

The next morning, we tried to plea out the case Phyll was worried about and the Assistant DA, Edward Stevens, would not agree to shit, so I set it for a jury trial.

I then drove to Houston and took a Southwest Flight to Dallas and went to the Financial Office where Pastor Shutte said his son worked. I didn't call in advance and I was glad afterward. I might not have had the nerve. Pastor Shutte's son owns the company he works for, which bears his name Roger Shutte Investment Counselor and his office is situated in a ten-floor tower he owns. He is an extremely handsome, well-preserved, knowledgeable and seemingly successful man.

"I am not here for financial guidance," I explain shaking his hand. "I am Alexandra McLeod. I am a lawyer doing primarily criminal defense by appointment of the Court for largely indigent people. I do not make enough money to consider investment; but I am impressed enough with your operation to consider changing my mind if you allow people to start very small."

"I can open an account for one share if I have to," he says. "And if you listen to me, I can double that often enough to make you glad that you did."

He is not bullshitting. He reeks of success and solidity. But he seems very down to earth and approachable.

"I just may do that," I say. "Tell me where to send the check and what information you need." I hand him my card.

"Okay, Ms. Alexandra McLeod," he says, taking my card and handing me his. "Why did you track me down and have my daddy call to let me know you were coming to see me?"

"I really didn't ask him to do that, but I did get an introduction to you because I am looking for someone that you knew very well. If I can't find her through you, perhaps I can find out about her from what you know."

He turns his chair away from me as if to say he does not want this to be happening and will shut me out; but when he reverses that process, he turns a level gaze on me.

"You are about to do what I have feared would happen for a long time and I just recently was able to put it aside and go on with the life I have. Just know that before you continue."

"I don't have a choice," I say and lay out my situation with the fact that my friend, Felipe Hernandez, also known as Fee Lo, and Babe are missing. I say he might have known her as Lorena Burnett, but I think she went as Babe for a long time.

"Since grade school," he says, shaking his head. "I know her as Babe."

"I believe somebody at Rutter Industries is engaging in dangerous activity. Babe is on to them, and it has put both of them in danger."

"How did he get involved?"

"Deputy Hernandez is a court deputy and friend of mine who lost his job; I believe she encouraged him to go to work there to help her get information. I fear they are both in danger."

He listens attentively and then I can almost feel the wheels turning as he considers what I have said and turns to his computer and starts typing in terms.

"What you say about this situation appears to have some validity," he says and turns back to face me.

"Tell me what happened in so far as you know."

"In so far as I know," I say. "My friend, who sometimes helps me on cases is Felipe Hernandez. He was a Deputy for the County Sheriff, who provides law enforcement to the Court System. He is quite enamored with Babe."

Roger Shutte sits back as if to absorb this.

"I know Babe was working on something at Rutter," I say. "It's a feeling more than something supported by direct proof, that she somehow enticed Fee Lo into it. I know he went to Rutter and applied for a job. I know because he took my car and left me his motorcycle to drive, which is something he habitually does and has for some time."

Roger Shutte reacts to this with a smile. "I can't picture that," he says.

"Don't worry about it," I say. "Driving a motorcycle is not something I do every day—just when he sticks me with his."

"No, it's an interesting idea to contemplate," he explains. "I've never done it. Now I might," he says, smiling.

"Be careful, it can go South on you quickly," I say, laughing.

"Go on with your story," he says.

"Thank you. I went out there and talked to the Human Resources woman, who was very nice, but I could tell she was uncomfortable and that she was lying to me. She said she had not seen Fee Lo and didn't know who he was, but he told me about her. Described her to a T and said he had a wonderful time just having coffee with her and that he got the job. She took him around and introduced him to the people who had to say yes."

"She still said no. She didn't know him."

Roger Shutte looks off toward a painting on his wall. It's a West Texas scene. A ranch, complete with a windmill and an oil well.

"And he and Babe have disappeared," I say. "I am trying to find people who knew her well enough to know where she might have disappeared to and I am probably overreacting, but I feel the danger."

He turns to his computer, types in a few more things and studies the screens that pop up.

"I do investments," he says, after a considerable silence. "I came up with an app that provides the basis for much of my advice. It gives me information on entities that folks are interested in. I'm not interested in sharing my methods with you or how I do what I do.

"I do have people who invest in Rutter. It's a very successful operation and they have interests worldwide. They have about 40,000 direct employees plus about 120,000 independent contractors in sixty different countries. They are worth at least one hundred billion dollars."

"That's a lot of money," I say.

"Such a lot it is powerful," Shutte says, "and they don't risk losing it or the power." He agrees and goes back to his screens. He strolls through what appear to be photographs of Rutter and its operation. "Satellites are wonderful," he says, "we can go all over the world without leaving our chairs. There's a little down time, because they are dated, but come around and look at this," he invites me to come behind his desk but swings his computer screen so we can both see. "Is that out of the glare?" he asks.

"I can see well," I say.

"Here's the layout at Rutter," he zooms out and the entire plant spreads out and fills his screen. It is a massive complex along the Gulf of Mexico. Then he zooms in and points to a place where fences lead to gates that are closed and governed by a booth that seems occupied. "Twenty-four hours a day," he says. "That booth is manned. No one goes in or out without passing through that gate.

Moving westward," he says as he moves the image with a little red light, "these are process areas where the primary life of the company, which is petroleum, is routed for the various by-products it goes into. This plant covers miles, not feet or yards. These miles stretch along the Texas coast, as you can see. This highway," he points to a line that hugs the coastline, "belongs to the State and everything between this line and water is public or private property. This long extension of water is the Intracoastal Canal. Commerce actually goes from East to West across the country for the duration of this waterway. It can no longer handle the bigger ships—they have to line up offshore, but this is Rutterport and Rutter owns most of it."

He pulls up another screen.

"This shouldn't mean much to you unless you have a habit of reading the most boring statistics in the world and most people don't; but this analysis is the heart of my operation," Shutte says.

"These graphs are what Rutter brings in each day. I don't have access to their internal documents so I don't know what they get from internal commerce, which is a lot, but I get enough from public transactions that I can make the predictions that I have to make to advise my clients. I guess I could get that information with the flick of a key, but frankly, I don't need or want the pressure that comes from hacking.

"I make opinions based on what they buy and sell on the open market and it works for me.

"Something strange must be happening right now at Rutter because it almost looks like two different operations. What do you see when I drag over everything on this West side of their operation?"

"I'm not sure I know what you are looking for," I concede.

"Well, try this?" He scans another area.

"This is the East side," he explains.

"Can you do that again?" I ask.

"I sure can; I want to see that again too. He drags the curser so that it moves slowly across the West field and then slowly to the East.

"Wow!" I say.

He nods agreement. "The sheer physical movement even in this satellite image tells me that recently something is happening on the East Side and that things are quiet to the point of sleep on the West."

He sits back and I return to the chair in front of his desk.

He looks at me for a long time.

Acts as if he wants to say something that he can't bring himself to do.

I want to say, what are you holding back, but I don't because I know that I need this man in my camp and for me, trust requires that you give each other time to put it in place.

"I would say that you should concentrate on what's going on in that East Field," he says. "That's where I see activity when there is relatively little elsewhere. The product purchases point climbs in the same direction, but I can't tell you yet what it may all be about. I will keep looking at it.

"The Old Maid portions of Rutter—the original work of the business—is almost at a standstill for activity. Almost like they sent everyone home. In that circumstance, the old men of the Board are more likely to go with an adventuresome activity on the other side, which I think is more associated with Research and Development, the coming up with new ideas. I've never seen that stark a contrast before. Usually that side would be moving and shaking and R&D would be a silent shell with only thinkers on the inside."

"And you know this how?" I ask.

"That's what I do for a living," he said. "Let me look at some other things." He goes back to his screen and dials up multiple things, reads them, deletes them and dials up more."

"Okay," he finally says. "You're right. Babe probably is onto something big, illegal and dangerous; and that is exactly where she would plant herself," he says. And he turns to me and grins. He is even more attractive when he grins.

"How do you do that," I ask. "You grin that way and I just fall head over heels in belief of everything you say?"

We both enjoy a good laugh.

"Miss Alexandra…"

I interrupt: "Call me Shadow, everybody else does."

"Shadow? I know there's a story there."

"A couple," I agree.

"I was a tent preacher from the time I was 12-years-old and up 'til Babe spirited me away from the true faith. My Preacher Daddy has never forgiven her and never will. She turned a fool of a country boy into a rational and successful businessman by making me not be afraid to take a chance on life. She convinced me that I did not have to be afraid of God and retribution and all of those fearful consequences of sin that marked our days growing up in the clutches of fundamentalist religion because if there is a God, He or She understands, Babe says. If He or She made us in their image, They love us, and if They created us to be different, that has to be part of the Grand Plan. I have never loved a woman quite in the same way that I love Babe. I say love haltingly and should do so in the past tense because if she walked in that door today, I don't think I would go with her, but I would still want to."

"Wow!" I say and I am grateful that he has made me a witness to the level of intimacy he just revealed. "Thank you," I add. "I was so afraid that Babe had done something really, really cruel to you. Like after using you, leaving you to fend for yourself."

"Oh, she did that all right too," he says, "but she gave me a new life first." He looks at me long and seriously. "I would lay down my life for her; but I now have three little darling creatures that I have a vested interest in giving a perfect life to and I feel really grateful for that."

"So Babe taught you to live."

"In a word, you're right. I am enjoying this little true confession session and it is a pleasure to have met you; but I have some appointments," he says. "And I have to get back on my calendar. Let me run some programs that I have that try to spot where changes are taking place and how to meet them or exploit them. I will either make us rich, young lady, or I will rescue our Babe and your friend if he is with her."

He has the nicest grin and he spreads it wide for me and I feel like saying 'Halleluiah!' but I don't, of course. I take my leave and Uber back to Love Field and fly home.

When I tell Phyllis to send Roger Shutte a check for $500.00 for each of us to open investment accounts in both our names, she balks.

"I knew it was a mistake for me to let you go off alone," she says, flipping the check she has taken from the checkbook back and forth against her wrist.

"You missed out, for sure," I tell her. "Roger Shutte is the real thing. I am so excited about meeting him."

"Is he married?" she asks, which is always her first consideration about men.

"Permanently bound," I say. "Wife and three kids he adores. Says his little one is just like Babe. You just don't understand," I say, unable to tell my God-fearing assistant that Roger Shutte crossed the divide. He found a way to believe in a loving God; but not to let it ruin his life.

I do tell her how much Roger Shutte still loves Babe for leading him out of the darkness and bringing him the reward of intellectual satisfaction. While she said no to discipline and school, she forced his way through SMU before she left to chart her own course.

"You don't have to worry about Babe," he said to me as I was leaving. "Because of the things that happened to her as a child, she is always going to be a risk-taker. She's immune from fear. She'll win in the end. I hope your friend Fee Lo is as lucky," he says.

"Any idea who she might contact if she got in real trouble?" I asked.

"I would hope me, but I don't think so now. She virtually ordered me to find a conventional woman and fall in love with her and have a normal life that was not possible for her. She knows I did that. I don't think she'll risk doing damage to my personal life. Babe has more character in her pinkie finger than most people do in their whole bodies. I will never let anyone say the contrary, even my Daddy, whom I love dearly and know is a good and well-intentioned man; but he's wrong about Babe. She didn't take my life. She gave it back to me after I had been used in ways that could have been psychologically devastating. She made it wonderful.

"When I was 12 and the darling of fundamentalism, I could scream and quote scripture and pray like the big boys. Babe fell in line with me. She would sing and hit the tambourine and literally dance to the music and those people loved us and threw money at us like circus clowns.

"I had hair you would not have believed. A pompadour that rose six inches to the glory of God and I was as sincere as a kid could be. Babe let hers grow real long and kept it straight as a board and her face was as clean of make-up as the wind-driven snow.

"And one day she looked at me and said: 'Rog, I can't do this anymore. I've become a caricature of all the things I don't like.'

"But what would we do?' I asked her. "You know what she said?"

"No," I admit.

"Anything honest."

"And we did. I told my Daddy not to follow me or try to bring me back. It was over. And I know he cried for weeks thinking I was gonna slide right then deep into the fires of hell. And perhaps I should have. But Babe brought me to Dallas and dressed me up and enrolled me in SMU in the business program. The rest is history."

He gave me his own card on which he had written two names and jotted down two numbers.

"If it's insight you want," he said. "Next to me, these two people knew Babe best."

Phyll reads Roger's bio on the Internet and looks at the size of his company, and says hump; but I know that she's impressed. He supports all the causes she does and he's able to do that without limiting his own life.

I tackle my files with a new energy, knowing that some of us do the things we want to do for the people we want to help and the money be damned. I believe Roger Shutte's next life should be as an inspirational teacher. I felt changed just being with him that short time.

"What'd he say about Rutter?"

"He's gonna call you when he gets what he's looking for," I say. "He seems to know what he's doing. I told him you would know what to do with it."

She seems momentarily satisfied. I have put her back in the driver's seat.

CHAPTER NINE
High School Days

The next day I do my docket as quickly as I can and head back up to Kilgore, in Phyllis' car this time. I take Lavern a box of Voo Doo donuts, which she found delightful!

"Oh, my goodness girl, what on earth. Just look at those!"

I ask her about Babe's school experiences, which she admits she knew very little about. Education was not something the family considered important, especially for girls.

I go to the high school and introduce myself to the principal, a nice young woman with fluffy blonde hair. She says she can't give out personal information about teachers and I tell her I was referred by Roger Shutte.

Shutte's name is magic.

"Oh, Mr. Shutte sent you," the Principal rationalizes to greet me differently. Apparently, he has the money to endow college scholarships for every local child in the high school who is accepted to a college.

"He provides a scholarship for the first year in college at the college that accepts them," she says, "but tells them they must come up with a plan before he will take on the other three years.

"We don't have many students going up," she says. "But so far, he is batting 100 percent for keeping those who get accepted in school until they graduate."

I know by that point that she is talking herself into an exception. I didn't know that until the day is over.

"I can call them," she says. "If they agree, I'll tell you how to find them. Both are retired."

Miss Jean Newman is a retired English teacher. According to Roger Shutte, she maintained excellent rapport with Babe.

"You have to understand," Miss Newman says when she lets me into the white, glass-paned door to her Queen Anne Cottage. "Babe was not a student. She was too busy living life and too ambitious to slow down for school. She was just not a good academic student. No patience. She frustrated her other teachers but not me, because I saw something in Babe that was precious.

"For one thing, she had an absolutely horrible situation at home. She came to the school nurse about it, but in those days, we didn't do anything if the abuser was family, because these families are hard to hold together anyway.

"I knew Babe would go somewhere; I just could not calculate where or how because she had nothing and no back-up.

"But she was strong. So determined. So ambitious."

"Yes," I nod in agreement. "She still is."

"It breaks my heart to think that someone could hurt her—she went through more than any child should have to bear and she held her head high through it all.

"She knew none of that was about her," Newman says. She gets really quiet and looks outside her window at a blooming tree that looks encrusted with orchids. The South knows it as a tulip magnolia but I am just meeting it for the first time. It is exceedingly beautiful.

"As a teacher, that's how you know you are looking at a survivor," she says, returning her look my way.

"Her Mother was pathetic even then. She has a chronic lung condition. She should not have lasted this long having a man that smoked right in her face that way. But Babe just let it go over her head. She knew her Mama could not do any more than she had."

"Didn't they pay her money when Babe's Daddy died that way?"

"Honey," she says to me. "This is East Texas. Other than comp benefits, do you think the lumber company thought about anything but itself? I'll bet they filed an insurance claim for their lost tree; but paid nothing to the widow and child. Claimed it was an act of God and not their negligence because nobody touched the tree before it fell."

"Tell me about her writing, please."

"Well, early on she had her voice pretty much established. I had to work on such things as syntax and grammar, which didn't interest her in the least. She would read her stories, some of them very personal, and the kids would actually clap when she threw in a dirty word. No one used words like fuck then, but Babe liberally sprinkled her work with such epithets and the class loved it.

"She learned that if she shocked them, they became her audience.

"You know when she got her Headliner's, she invited me to come and introduced me as the person that made writing available to her. It was one of my proudest moments."

"I loved her. She could have been my daughter in every respect but genes. And I had no children of my own."

I didn't want to leave Jean Newman; but I knew Phyllis was monitoring my time and that if I did not get back to be the last case on the docket, I would be in deep trouble with her.

I left Jean Newman with the feeling that I was finally getting into the heart of the real Babe; and my phone rang almost as soon as I got in the car. It was Edward Stevens, First assistant to District Attorney Frieda Henny.

"Miss McLeod," he says. "Phyllis MacArthur tells me you are in Deep East Texas doing the Lord's work. She says you need a reset on the Bullard case.

"Maybe," I say. "Depends on what you might be inclined to offer if I can delay it another week."

"What I offer depends on where you intend to go with the case."

"You know me," I say, openly flirting with this man that I am admittingly attracted to. "Figure out what I want and give it to me or I'll feel forced to go to trial."

"This case does not need to be tried," he says. "I'll roll it over and you come by when you get back in town."

"I'll be there for sure tonight," I say and start to hang up but he hurries to add: "Tonight would work fine for me."

"How are you gonna get the judge to stay?" I tease.

He laughs. "We might make a better deal without her," he says and I put a little sultry tone in my voice and say: "I'll call you."

I admit my heartbeat jumps a little.

Floyd Conner is a coach. He was the high school coach and coached it all: Football. Basketball. Golf. Tennis. Track. Wrestling. His wall shows he had one team in each that went to State at least once but only one to win, he told me when I diplomatically asked how they did, the girl's volleyball team went and Babe made the final winning point.

"Came off the bench to make a penalty point. I never used anybody but her for that and there was no changing it in that game.

"In basketball, Babe was a standout player who could not dribble the ball enough to move it down court. She was not in any sense of the imagination an athlete. She did not like to run because she didn't like to sweat. But, she practiced penalty points every day during practices and scrimmages and games and any other time when she knew better than to go home.

"I showed her how to trip the back door to the gym so she could come in and stay over when it actually wasn't safe for her to go home. People knew that old man was doing what he ought notta been doing to her, but the only solution was to ignore it and keep her out of his reach. Her Mama was on welfare. Babe was like a foster child of everybody that knew her. Even old Preacher Shutte. Kicked himself ten times over for the way it turned out."

Floyd Conner started laughing.

"That's probably the biggest irony I ever heard of in my life. Shutte's not yet forgiven her for taking his son out of the tent, but she pushed him into a position to be able to support that old man's church, which he does, and I don't think the daddy even suspects it. If we have any brains at all out here, Roger Shutte sends it to college. He has probably upgraded the mental acumen of this community more than any other person because some of these people actually come back here to live and work.

"Babe was the pretty little girl without a single boyfriend. I thought it was self-induced and that she would have a hard time ever thinking about getting married. But she was always steady and had her feet on the ground.

"I couldn't put her in the game because it would have been a disaster. But if the game turned on penalty points, it was up to her and we would win. I always had to be careful and know when it was all right to put her in. For one thing, she never wanted the other side to lose but she didn't want her team to lose either. She was toned and used athletics to burn off steam and anger. But throwing that basketball through the basket was the only thing she could do well in sports and she did it top notch."

"I'm glad you came to see me," he tells me. "I haven't thought about Babe for a while now. We see Roger every year at least once but nobody has the courage to ask him about Babe. You can tell it still hurts too much."

Floyd Conner said when I got there, he'd been up and cooking a brisket for twelve hours and the odor has permeated the small ranch-style house in which he is spending retirement.

"You're gonna have to excuse me, Young Lady, because my nose is beginning to tell me it's time to take out that brisket."

"I can go," I say.

"No, no," he replies. "You got a rare chance in your life today to have some Floyd Conner baked brisket and you don't want to miss out on that."

"You're right I don't," I say and he takes out the brisket, peels back the foil in which he wrapped it, and lets the meat rest while he pours off the juice that runs out. I offer to help but he says no, it's easier to get the things done than tell someone else where to find the tools and how to do the work. He gathers white bread that looks homemade, onion slices in a zip lock bag in the refrigerator, pickles from a crock on the counter and two plates.

"It was a feast," I tell Phyll later, while she samples the left-overs he pressed me to bring to her.

"I'm jealous," she admits. "Tomorrow you have to do the courthouse run and make peace with Eddie Stevens, and I will do the traveling." She laughs but I know she's not kidding."

"Actually, I was going to suggest that," I lie and she grins. "I want you to revisit Lavern and ask her whatever happened to the family of Babe's daddy and about whatever happened to her second husband. I would like for you to make sure that phone is working and that Laverne knows how to work it. I know Babe put it there for a reason and it wasn't just so her Mother could reach out to her."

"I can do that," Phyllis says.

"And then I wonder if you could go see Preacher Shutte and see what kind of things he has around the house from the old tent revival days. It may not lead us anywhere, but I kinda believe there had to be a musician or two behind the scenes if they were able to do what Roger says they did so successfully."

CHAPTER TEN
Shadow Meets Townsend

The next morning I sit across from Edward Stevens at about eight. Phyll is correct: he is an early riser.

"That was easy," I say as he accepts my request for probation in the custody of the DA and dismissal if Ballard satisfies all the requirements. He agrees to go on possession and six months. Phyllis will give me an A because she is worried about this case. Ballard and his family go to her Church.

"You must be in a better mood early in the morning than after you've been in court for a couple hours."

"Aren't we all?" he asks and takes a long swallow of coffee from an oversized Starbuck's cup. It dribbles onto his white shirt and he wipes it off, leaving a stain. He yawns and leans back in his chair.

"And not enough sleep," I surmise.

"Not enough," he said. "I stayed up waiting for your call."

"Sure," I say, thinking he was surely kidding, and I slip my own cup from my shoulder-bag, brief case to join him in coffee, thinking we will work out the details, but it seems to be done.

"Will you tell the clerk to get the papers and I will get his family down?"

"Sure," he says and gives detailed instructions to whoever is on the phone. I repack my brief case while he does this and I stand. He motions with his hand for me to stay.

When he gets off the phone he says: "Are you getting what you need on Rutter?"

"Somewhat," I say. "I met an incredible man who told me more in sixty seconds that I've been able to find on the Internet. He's promised to look at some other aspects for me."

"Local?" he asks.

"East Texas," I say. "Dallas now. You ever heard of Roger Shutte, a financial adviser?"

"Don't think so," he says.

"Local boy who made really good," I say.

"I asked around about Rutter after you asked me the other day. You might want to go talk to Jim Townsend at the *Enterprise*. He knows Rutter and Babe. I think he can help you. He said he'd be glad to talk to you."

"Thank you. Thank you very much. I really do appreciate the help."

"For you, Miss McLeod, nothing is a bother."

I smile as I leave him because he is blushing.

When I get back to the office, Phyllis thanks me for the outcome on her case by phone from Kilgore. I can tell she is deep in her "investigative mode," when I reach her.

"You better set up a support group for that one, Phyll. He was there with his parents. I don't know about them but he could be in deep trouble if he messes up on this."

"I'm on it," she promises and we hang up and go back to our respective tasks, mine to pull out my Babe notes and go to the *Enterprise* to see Jim Townsend.

"It was good of you to see me," I say.

"Glad to do it," the *Enterprise* Editor and General Manager says. "I want that reporter found as much as you want your friend Hernandez to be found. I want them both to be okay."

"Edward Stevens seemed to recall that the *Enterprise* has a history with Rutter. Can we talk about that?"

"Rutter has always been our biggest advertiser and its contributions to the City are not matched by anyone or any other entity. You could almost call this City Rutterville and you wouldn't be too far off. Clinics, Hospitals, Parks, Schools, Libraries, Civic Centers, Neighborhood Meeting Centers, Senior Citizen Activity Halls, a building in every Commissioner's Precinct for local activities. All have Rutter's touch. And, in exchange, they want tax exemptions, which if you gave them a deduction for what they have paid out, might not hurt, but their income is so enormous that the tax bill, if accurately levied, is far above that."

"I discovered that it should be in the millions," I say.

"Multi," he says. "But what they want, they are accustomed to getting. I believe the relationship tends to create a void where good government gets lost. The City supported us and the *Enterprise* took the editorial position that the County ought to bill Rutter for its fair taxes and then build its own public facilities. Neither the City nor the County should be taking handouts from a single taxpayer and then be told what to do in return. But it was not a popular position.

"Until people heard what Rutter should be paying, and a sizeable group started leaning in favor of the *Enterprise*'s position. What Rutter was saving in taxes, alone, was far greater than Rutter's costs in building infrastructure for the City and people began to see we could have better streets and roads and street lights and even trolleys if Rutter was required to meet its obligation and some of the incentives were passed around to other businesses that can't compete with Rutter now.

"Well," he adds. "It almost put us out of business. We lost Rutter advertising. We lost some public advertising. The Commissioners, who liked having the Rutter incentives in their own areas—you know what they are, large streamline senior centers, buses, barns, SUVs and so on—even withdrew public notice ads for a time and published handbills and posted them around the courthouse and on the light posts.

"It was war."

"And the person who stirred this sleeping giant?" I ask.

"Well Babe started it. She had a friend somewhere, who fed her the information; and it was impeccable and totally accurate."

I could see Roger Shutte's hand in play and guessed that, despite his protests to the contrary, they maintained contact. Perhaps I need to talk to him again.

Or, maybe I would send Phyllis and she would no longer be pissy about my time with Roger and our investment.

Townsend and I talked for nearly an hour.

He talked.

I listened.

And at the end I was beginning to see a pattern. Rutter has it in for Babe and Babe has it in for Rutter.

"You might call Dr. David Dickerson," Townsend tells me. "He was at Rutter for a long time. He might be hard to find. The word is that Rutter black-listed him."

"I expect my assistant will be able to find him," I say. "She has the nose of a bloodhound."

"What do you think has happened to Babe and your friend?" he asks me finally.

"I have two theories not for publication," I say. "Confidentially, I feel they are either in dire circumstances against their will or the two of them have things fully under control and are successfully hiding."

"Let's hope it's the latter," he says and shakes my hand.

CHAPTER ELEVEN
Finding the Musician

Phyll is elated with her day of investigation!

She not only found a picture, from Pastor Shutte's papers on his son's tent revival days, showing Roger as a young charismatic preacher and Babe with her tambourine. But she holds it away from me to keep something as a surprise.

"You were right," she says, pointing toward a long-haired fella with a guitar strap around his neck, jeans, a long vest that actually has leather ribbons tied in the end that reach his knees and are captured flowing around him from the movement of his body as he plays. They are all the same age and beautiful in their youth.

"His name is Ronald Tucker but he actually went around as RonTon, the Holy Roller, then. He's a one-man act.

"After spending the time it took with Pastor Shutte, I couldn't get to Ron Ton—he is in New Orleans anyway; and he has dropped the Holy Roller. Does a new thing, he said. I did talk to him, he said he'd talk to you, but that he would call you when he has time. He also needed to think about whether he wants you to reopen wounds.

"I have to tell you. My impression is that he is still a latter-day flower child, caught in a stage he can't go forward from. He expresses out and out anguish in a very dramatic way."

"You have to go there—I don't mean go to New Orleans—you just have to talk to him yourself. If you believe him, let me know."

"I'll let him call me first. You think we're opening up too many sensitive hearts? We don't have any right to do that, I don't think."

"Except that neither one of us has any ability to walk away. Even if it is flippant little Fee Lo, Damn him!"

I form a half-laugh; but it won't come out.

I look over the notes she made and the photographs, two or

three of which are very interesting and then slip them aside and start looking at the files.

"I can't think," I say apologetically, "I am losing my frigging mind. I've got to stop worrying about that man and get some work done."

"What did you find out?" she asks me.

"Nothing. I went back out to Rutter and went through the front gate. I asked that Dude if Fee Lo had come in yet. He is security, after all, and he gave me a blank face. I told him I had an appointment with Sharon Donaldson and he confirmed it before he let me in. She apparently told him I had an appointment and he let me in. I expected more. She seems like the nicest woman ever. But she gave me this blank stare and said, 'No, I've never seen him. I wish you could understand. I can't make somebody up when he's never been here.' She is either a colossal liar or he is."

"Well, you know the odds there."

"I guess. But he's never done this before."

"Not exactly like this but his track record, you have to admit, is full of disappearances on us."

"Little things, Phyll. Going off for a weekend with a new woman. "Till Babe that is."

"Yeah, you're right there. He was always reachable too."

"I'm convinced something's wrong. That woman was so nervous. Even the assistant, when I threw out McNelly's name, took a deep breath."

"You did that?"

"What?"

"Used McNelly's name?"

"What else could I do? I had to get a rise from him some way."

"Fee Lo at least told you to stay away from anything close to Jack McNelly."

"Did he?"

"Maybe not. Maybe I've heard that name from somewhere else."

I take a step back into my office and turn around. "When I'm on the alert, do you react in the same way?"

I got a long incredulous stare over glasses she is trying out for proof-reading. Then she smiles. "Of course, I do. Why?"

"What are you thinking or feeling about all of this?"

"I think you should go see Doctor Alice. It's just too much in a long string. Maybe you need to work out how you feel about Fee Lo?"

"What do you mean, how I feel about him?"

"Maybe this is love," Phyllis shares.

"Of course it's love; but its love a mother feels when a child is threatened by danger," I say. "The chemistry I have with Fee Lo is love for sure; but not in love if you know what I mean."

"That's why I have Doctor Alice," she says. "She always points me in the right direction."

"No you talk it out and work it out for yourself. I know how that works," I tell her. "I send a lot of people to therapy!"

CHAPTER TWELVE
Sharon Calls

She called at four as a collect call from a pay phone. She called me Aunt Rose and did not identify herself. Her voice had such urgency that I followed her instructions and called her back on one of Phyll's throw-down-prepaids. She sounded like a typical overly threatened woman whose husband had just been hauled off to jail.

"He threatened me," she says, barely able to get the words out. "He's over the top!"

"First tell me who," I tell her. "And try to be calm. You're going to be okay."

"McNelly," she says and I am no longer as sure.

"Was that what happened after I left?" I ask. "Was that when it happened?"

I gave her directions to our office.

"Can you go with me to my Mother's house?" she asks.

"I hate to use the language he used," Sharon Donaldson says. "But as soon as you left my office, he came in and clenched his hands on my face and said: 'How did that Bitch get my name, Sweet Little Sharon Donaldson?' Jack McNelly is a real scary man, and he keeps his voice at an even whisper, but the anger escapes through those clenched teeth."

"I don't know," I told him and pulled my face away from his hands. "You touch me like that again, and I will file formal charges against you."

"'You won't, Sweet Thing,' he told me. 'You'll never get the chance."

"That's against the law," I said, as if that would stop him.

"He laughed at me."

"No, it's against the law to go against the interests of your employer and make irrational charges against a trusted executive."

"You are no trusted executive here, Sir,' I said. But he went around my desk and sat down. By that time I was struggling to draw an even breath, but I stared him down."

"Don't forget who interviewed you for this position and who explained your job duties to you as fully as they could be explained when you replaced the retiring Human Resources Director' was what he said."

"Pushed out, he was," I said, attempting to stay strong.

"If you know what's good for you," he says. "You'll remember your job. If I tell you a matter that comes before you is confidential and privileged, remember what that means. You don't know it exists. You've never seen it. You don't tell Little Mexican Security Guards about it and you don't tell their weeping women anything when they come looking for him.'"

He then said awful, personal things to me. Said when you fed me Felipe's line all over again, I creamed like a virgin,' and I pushed him out of my office, with him laughing at me all the way.

"He's a bully: 'I will get out when I damn well please, Miss Donaldson,'" he said. "'When I damn well please!'"

"When he looked back at me from my door, he paused and looked back from the door like he was sending a warning. "And don't look for your taping system, when I leave your office. In case you had not guessed, I took yours out and installed a much better two-way that plays right out in my office. You can't get away from my eyes or ears. I hear and see everything you say and do."

"Then he slammed my door behind him," she says, tears flowing.

Sharon Donaldson gives me directions to her Mother's house and then says, she will come by here and lead us there. When she reaches our office, the first thing she does is grab a Kleenex Box that is on Phyllis' desk in our entry area of the office and I think it is to wipe her face, because she has cried so much her eyes are swollen and red and her face looks saturated. But she digs her fingers into the box and reaches around inside it, looking stunned.

"He threw mine away," she said, this time openly sobbing. "I dug the box from the trash, actually looking for my cell phone, which I thought I had set to record but it was no longer where I put it."

Shaking, she leans back in her chair and swivels her body around to look out my front window.

"My office overlooks the stacks in East Field," she says. "Rutter is as busy as ever, but something has changed to cause such drama. Everyone who reports to me for East Field has started stepping aside when they see me coming. They dodge my questions and draw slow, stealthy, circles around me when they come by to turn in their time. It's almost as if I am now cursed. Twenty-five years I have been a fair-haired girl at Rutter and now nobody speaks to me.

"Something has happened to the new security guard.

"I am afraid to ask but your friend Fee Lo was there and I hired him, and when he asked, I sent him to the East Field and he disappeared. McNelly would not tell me for sure; but I saw him going into areas he was denied access to and I did not warn him. What on earth is going on that would set McNelly off that badly?"

Sharon takes a note pad from her purse as she said she did that night and shows me her record of McNelly's threats, a few scribbled short notes to set the time and date on which he had threatened her and squeezed her face with his hands.

"I put the note with your card in my purse, closed it and took it with me to the coffee shop. And then I left and I came here. I need your help."

I look at Phyllis and she is shaking as openly as Sharon is.

CHAPTER THIRTEEN
Phyll the Home Nurse

We get the address and I follow Sharon's instructions and drive behind her from a distance. "I'm being followed," she warns us; but I can't tell if anyone is behind us. I did not come alone. I am not really a brave person.

I introduce Phyllis to Sharon Donaldson's Mother as a Home Healthcare Nurse, who is doing practice hours and needs a patient.

Phyll, bless her heart, as Millie used to say of the persevering in life, rose to the occasion.

"Come with me, Dear, Let's see how things are going," Phyll says, leading Mom into another room to get to know her and practice her trade. The interview, when I looked at it was actually pretty professional, better than most probably; and it looks once more as if Phyll can be dropped into any situation, and she just plods right through to success.

"Baptist upbringing," she always says.

"Ten years of being a youth counselor," I say, "Nothing ever surprises you!" It doesn't and no person is beneath her; she is a true common denominator.

Meanwhile, Sharon pulls out some files that she has been copying and bringing home to her Mother's house. She tells us that what has been happening at Rutter since Jack McNelly came on the scene is not like any other busy time at Rutter. She has never seen so many people laid off on one side and pumped up with strangers on the other. These newcomers have no records and include some from strange lands.

"I have no prejudice in my heart," she says, "but I know they speak no English because they never understand what I am saying to them."

She hands me a scrap of paper that shows how they report their hours.

"I hand them the cash, which is the way that entire job has been funded.

"Then Dr. David Dickerson went missing," she says.

"He came through my office one night, motioned me to be silent. Took my bag into the bathroom and when he came back he left and I never saw him again; and I spent an hour with McNelly with him telling me what I knew that I didn't. I fully expected him to strike me then, but he didn't.

"After that Miss Burnett vanished."

"Babe," I asked? "How did you know she was gone?"

"He told me again. We had another session in which he said he knew that I knew. But she was gone, and I didn't know where or why, although he thought I knew and kept saying why and where is she."

She pulls out a file and hands it to me.

"I don't think I can keep this safe anymore," she says; "and I think it's a danger to my Mother for it to be here. Dr. Dickerson wrote me this note. Read it.He looked at me so seriously that I knew it was important. He trusted me to keep this safe. And then he was gone."

I look down at the note. The Doctor wrote: "The safety of the whole world depends on your getting this to the right people." One part of me wanted to scream at him. The nerve to do this to an innocent woman. The other part scared me as much as this woman was scared.

"So what did you do?" I ask.

"The same thing I did with you," she says. "I called the FBI. I couldn't tell them about Dr. Dickerson's papers although they asked me a lot of questions and then said I needed to call the local police. I made a bad mistake. I sent your Fee Lo to the East Field to see if he could find out what was going on. He never came back."

And there we were.

She unloads and feels better. I feel her anguish crossing right over to me. And what do I do? I pat her on the arm.

My Mother's gesture.

I frankly am torn. I don't want this problem.I want to get up. Pretend it never happened. And go home.

Then Phyllis comes to the door.

"Miss McLeod," she says, very formally. "I need to put my patient to bed and to make sure Miss Sharon is going to be with her for the night. She's very upset because she can tell Sharon is upset. Can I ask you to stay with her tonight?"

"I always stay with her," Sharon says. "This is where I live."

"I guess I mean would you be willing to sleep in there with her? I don't know what happened to her today, but she's very upset."

"Of course," Sharon says apologetically. "I'll let you two out and I'll be right here. Don't worry. She will be okay."

"I hated so much to lie to you about all this," she says wiping tears at the door. "I did interview Felipe. It was wonderful just to spend that time with him. He's quite a young man. But someone, I have to guess, McNelly, stole his file. And he's gone. Disappeared during the night shift."

At this point she breaks down completely.

"There's a rumor they hung him!"

"What do you mean?" I am whispering a scream at her.

"They say that every time someone goes AWOL out there."

"At Rutter?"

"East Field. Rutter is a dear old place, and I mean that the good way. I've been there 25 years—ever since high school. We've never had this drama ever. But someone did get hanged once and they said it was a suicide. It wasn't."

"What do they actually make there?"

"Depends on where you are," she says. "Rutter pretty much does it all. Construction. We build those refineries. Chemicals. We process oil, petroleum, its by-products. Plastics. Then we transport it by truck and pipeline. Finance. We do everything for everybody on credit most of the time. I don't know of anything that we don't do. Our charity side even builds schools in Nicaragua and Costa Rica and any other place we want to put a factory.

"Pretty much everything.

"Everywhere for everyone.

"We are much better at being a business than you'd believe with this McNelly person and I can't find out anything about him. He just doesn't exist before the day he walked in the door and took over. Poor Jim."

"Who is Jim?" I ask.

"Just my former boss. He was a great, decent guy. McNelly pushed him right out in a matter of hours and took over."

"You're right. Something doesn't seem right about that."

"And I dumped Felipe right in the middle of it," she says, breaking out in a new flood of tears.

I did my best to calm her down and keep her talking.

"Jack McNelly is an evil man," she tells me. "It almost seems like he can cross through walls. If you try to do anything, even go into the restroom to make a call, he appears outside the stall. It's as if he can look right through walls and skin and bone and know what you are thinking."

"Do you have any idea why?"

"No. If I did I would tell you so you could tell someone else. He knows we are talking right now and I'm sure he knows what we are saying?"

"And you have no idea what's happening or where at the plant Fee Lo might have gone that he should not have?

"Oh I know that. It's the Southeast field, right outside my office. People have to walk through my office and I have to see their id before they can walk out of my office and go into the East Field. You can see it from the highway that runs just North of the Blue Water Highway."

"Do you have a list of these approved employees?"

"I can make one. It's been going on long enough for me to know a few of them by first name when they walk in."

"Let's do so," I say. We close the door and Phyllis gets out a notebook and starts writing. She starts giving me names, all male, of people working in this highly monitored area called the East Field. I write them down as she spells them. Some are just plain West Texas names but a few are Hispanic. Some Asian. And a sprinkling sound as if they come from the Middle East.

"Any idea why the project area is so 'closed' with your office functioning as the only access in and out."

"None," she says. "I know that reporter was messing around too."

That figures, I am thinking. Of course Babe got Fee Lo into this. And she found out something, I am sure.

Sharon and I talk into the night.

Long after Phyllis leaves us to answer Mom when she calls and puts her to bed. Long after Phyllis comes back in and sits with me and Sharon and even after Sharon tells Phyllis that yes, she approved the hiring of Fee Lo as a security guard and lied to me before.

Phyllis looks at me and her eyes get larger than quarters.

Sharon has no idea where McNelly came from or his intentions. As far as she is concerned it can't be good because he is evil to the core. She knows he is doing wrong with anything he would come up with and she has had nobody else to tell it to.

If Felipe trusted us, then she will too.

She repeats for Phyllis about when McNelly first showed up and how he just suddenly appeared out of nowhere and ran her boss off and repeated for her what her job is and what she does and the restraints.

Phyllis comforts her.

She turns to me: "I really need to know what Privileged and Confidential means in the law," she says.

I explain to her that under Laws of Privilege recognized by many States in their rules and laws, confidences made to doctors, psychiatrists, lawyers, ministers and among co-workers in some circumstances, who are performing confidential work for their employers, can be protected and not revealed. But privilege cannot be used to cover up a crime, even when the confidence is made to a psychiatrist if it is likely to lead to a crime or bring harm to another person, the psychiatrist must reveal it to the authorities.

"But what could we be doing at Rutter that would require such secrecy?" she asks.

"Well it could be any kind of intellectual property. Companies do research and development to stay alive and be competitive. If they publish what they are doing, then it's not easy to patent what ultimately the company or its people discover or develop."

"It doesn't seem right that they can cause people to disappear under some rule of privileged and confidential activities," she says.

"Unfortunately, there's a difference between something being right and something being legal," I say. "But privilege does not give you a right to commit a crime to protect your privilege. This McNelly seems to be really messed up."

"I have to go back to work," she tells me. "I've never been afraid before at Rutter. It's like my family. But I'm all my Mama has."

"You've got to protect yourself," I say. "Who's in charge of Security out there?"

"That's just it," she says. "I hired Felipe as additional security for the East Field and no one can tell me whatever happened to him," she says. "Security guards just look at me with an empty face now."

She looks at Phyllis: "I need your promise, Miss Phyllis, that you will get somebody to protect my Mother if something happens. She will be lost if I don't show up regularly."

I look through the file she has given me. Page after page of math problems, it looks to me. Maybe the hardest test ever written in fact. Mixed in with the figures are things I recognize from college chemistry that I recognize only because I had to hire a tutor who advised me to get through Chemistry as best I could by memorizing the periodic elements table and to stay away from it after that. He taught me his own formula for memorizing the Periodic Table and I tried to find significance in the symbols I saw.

"Did you understand this?" I ask Sharon.

"No, not a line of it."

"Tell me about Dr. Dickerson." I was curious now because I'd heard his name two times in the same week. Jim Townsend knew him and referred me to him. Now I realize that he didn't tell me where or how to find him and, apparently, he did not know Dickerson was now also among the missing.

"I want you to take that. You must have a safe you can put it in."

I am thinking that I surely do; but I don't think it's good enough to beat a Rutter assault. I do have a safety security box at Moody Bank for the Deed to my house that General reluctantly signed and decide maybe that is strong enough to ward off a Rutter attack.

"Can you take your Mama and leave town?" I ask Sharon Donaldson. "And not tell anybody where you are going?"

She looks at me sadly.

"The only support we have is Rutter. I am a 9 to 5 worker. This man wants to be rid of me."

"I think I can keep you safer, easier if you agree to leave."

"I can't. I'm not a quitter. This man is trying to ruin my life and my livelihood. I am the only support my mama has. I think it would kill her to leave this house. I can't do that to her. She is in a fragile state now anyway."

I look Sharon Donaldson over carefully. Her resolve seems resolute and however much I would like to hide her out, I know I can't move her. She has been in charge of her world for a long time and I am not going to change that.

Outside, away from possible taps, I borrow one of Phyll's throw-downs and call Roger Shutte. True to my suspicion, when I explain to him this is my best clue yet to how to find Babe, he agrees to have someone meet me at the airport tomorrow.

I tell him I want to come see him about a private confidential matter and that I want to bring Phyllis with me.

Truly, I am getting us out of town as well until I can find out what's in this folder that Phyll and I copy that evening.

We put the original with my deed in the safety deposit box at Moody Bank the next morning as soon as the Bank opens and I use one of Phyll's throw-downs to photograph every page. We now have it in triplicate. If it really is something that will save the world, I think I have made enough copies to preserve it.

CHAPTER FOURTEEN
Roger Shutte, A Second Visit

"I've seen parts of this before," Roger Shutte says to me after he goes through my copy of the file with a great deal more understanding than I had been able to do.

"I know where you got it," I tell him. "That was somebody we both know was covering her tracks by filing duplicates. I believe that she might have stolen her copies. These are from a person I suspect knows the author of the formula well enough that he trusted her to put it in a safe place. He also must not have had anybody else."

"What I want to do," he says, "Just in case you were followed here. Babe has never put a foot in the door out there; but I could be her safe haven if she is in bad trouble. Her safe house, if you will, and I have a safe I've been stuffing things in for a long time now.

"Then what you told me about not having seen her since high school was not all together true," I say.

"Oh but it was. You didn't hear my subjunctive voice and qualifiers because you were taken with a person, who could have been a tent-preacher at 12, who now has a financial investment house that is one of the more successful in the country.

"I have an app," he says, "inspired by a pretty little girl with brown curls and blue eyes and I can't tell you how it works but it is patented and I've only let one entity use it besides myself.

"The FBI doesn't use it for the reasons I do, but we get our results. I want to run part of this through it and analyze what I think is here," Shutte says. "Your timing is good anyway, because I am just about to wrap up on the financial aspects of what is going on out there and I started that from Babe and what I was careful to tell you was that I have not talked to her since high school, but I know her well enough to know why she is sending me something when she does.

"Because my contact at the FBI is already working on this project, at this point, I have no option but to call them in and I want the two of you here when I do it. The primary reason is that I know you are not part of this. But the FBI might not trust you unless I vouch for you. I just wanted to tell you first. But I am not going to commit a crime or be part of a conspiracy to save Babe. I have too much at stake."

I look at Phyll, whose mouth is open and whose breath is coming in irregular gusts.

"Well you told me that meeting this guy was going to be different," she said. "That was your biggest understatement of the year."

He made us wait outside while he made his call. Of course, Phyll had some files for me to review, and I did so. I was due in court the next morning at 9 for a plea she had arranged and was not happy about. I planned to be there and try to sweeten the deal before the Judge took the bench. When he called us back in, a guy was sitting there in his office. Tall. Thin. White hat propped on the chair beside his. He looked up at me and grinned.

"I think we've met, Miss McLeod," he said. "I think I fished you out of the water and saved your life," he adds.

"And I think you get around," I say.

He laughs. I don't laugh because he is holding the copy of my file that I had let Roger Shutte review.

"I should have been clear, Mr. Shutte," I say, picking my file off the agent's knee. "This came to me as confidential information from a client. The fact that you are my advisory expert does not make it publishable to anyone else."

"That's obviously a Xerox copy," the lawman says.

"And the importance of that is?"

"Somebody has another copy. It's not the original."

I don't tell him that I have the original in a safe in Galveston.

"I don't think it matters, Sir," I say. "Respectfully, there are ways that you can get this; but this is not one."

"As you know Ms. McLeod, we have matched wits in Court and you slay the dragon better than anyone I've been questioned by so far. But unless you provide me with a copy of this document, I am going to ask my boss to bring charges against you for possessing it and you will not like the results."

Roger Shutte interrupts: "I didn't realize the two of you knew each other and had such an interesting experience history together; but as a tent-preacher I accomplished a lot of my prayer miracles by knowing how to read people. When I read the two of you, it's like looking at the end of a stick of dynamite after the wick is fired. Let me suggest a compromise that might help you both get past this pissing stand-off: I'm gonna read this stuff anyway, because I have other authority as well for part of it. I'm guessing here, but if I were a betting man I'd say neither one of you can tell heads from tails about it. Why don't you let me do my stuff and I'll call you both in, together, and we'll go over the results. How does that sound?"

The lawman looks at me.

"I can accept that," he says.

"I guess I can," I say.

I look at Phyllis, but I can tell from the look on her face that she sees another target; and thinks I have been withholding information.

"This is the gentlemen who pulled me out of Galveston Bay when I was pushed in by that fellow that followed us during the Bobby Gene trial," I tell her. "He's also the one you gave detailed directions to my house. Nothing more to the story."

"Now, Shadow, which you said I could call you, I want you to tell this officer about your client, because he is better able to help them than we are and your client is the link he's been looking for, I think."

So with Roger Shutte's urging, I sit down with Jacob Edgar Hoover, a tall and lanky FBI agent that I have met before on several occasions now and I tell him everything from Fee Lo's disappearance to Sharon Donaldson's visit and the delivery of the file. I remind myself as much as Phyllis when I explain this to her so that she will realize no strings attach to this guy. I don't care that he might be the most handsome man that I've ever seen, and for once a prospect that is taller than I am, and I must admit, Phyllis takes it all in stride.

Shutte urges me to seek FBI protection for Sharon Donaldson and I do so. It's pretty much established that my client will get better protection from the FBI than from Phyll and me; although they do not share with me the reason the FBI is willing to take over that responsibility. Shutte is also right about something else: When I met this lawman, he pulled me out of the water after a man we were both chasing jumped into Galveston Bay from the Galveston ferry, dragging me behind him. He caught my eye, even in the dark.

"Miss McLeod, I must say, you look even better up close in the daylight, even if you are still hostile to me for some reason."

In the light of day, in a plush office in Dallas, Texas, I can tell you he looked even better than I remembered too, but I don't give him that satisfaction.

The world seems too screwed up right now to have any romance in it.

"I remember you more from court," I say.

"Of course you would," he says, laughing. "You ate my lunch. I almost lost my job because I gave up my confidential informant to you on cross-examination. I haven't forgotten."

Phyllis looks from one to the other. She has that you-don't-fool-me-look on her face when she leans back in her chair and gives us both a once-over.

"I see I'm not needed here," she says. "Why don't ya'll talk, while I get myself a cup of coffee."

Phyllis and I get into scrapes all the time. It seems to be the thing we do best. We have done that before and we will do it again.

I finish up with the lawman and we agree to meet again when Shutte is ready and I go looking for Phyllis. She already has a cab at the front entrance and we barely make our flight back to Houston. She is on the phone as soon as we land and drives us straight to the courthouse.

CHAPTER FIFTEEN
Dr. Alice, I Presume

After our Dallas experience, for some reason, I am charged with energy. I get back to court and work my magic, as she calls it, and get the case pled. When I get back to the office, I am so wiped out, Phyllis makes me an appointment with her Dr. Alice and this time I go.

Dr. Alice looks like every family therapist that I have sent clients to and I'm not surprised that Phyll likes and depends on her. She is sweet, almost beyond belief, and has a proper psychological term that she shares after each major problem is discussed.

"For some reason," I tell her. "Seeing that guy I could really have the hots for in the middle of all this just throws everything into mental chaos for me. How low can I be to get that feeling, I admit, feeling like that when Fee Lo's missing and in danger? I asked myself, but I don't have an answer." I don't wait for the analysis.

"I have known Fee Lo for a few years now, almost all the time I've been in Texas," I tell Doctor Alice. "I came as a bride, and I was so excited about my new life with my own Prince Charming. He came here to teach. My Mama got me business with her early friends. I thought the world was my oyster and I its pearl.

"Boy was I wrong!

"My name is Shadow McLeod because I kept my maiden name as all responsible feminists do.

"The name fits. There always has been a cloud hanging over me. My own Mother said my true Father was a figment casting no shadows as he made his polite but quick exit as soon as he found out she was pregnant with me and was not about to get an abortion at forty!

So much for the source of the name.

"My Mother is still thrilled beyond belief that she has something to own: Me.

"My putative Father, the one who sent the support checks all those years, turned out not to be my Father at all; and I was both relieved and sad about that at the same time, if you can take it on faith for now. He is a piece of work, too. In fact of all the choices I had, and she admitted to several, not a one of these prospective fathers bears looking at twice from my standpoint because they've all been largely absent except that one who paid support, which you'd think he wouldn't have done had he not thought I was his kid. I spent the summer with him and his wife and children. There was a host of them and I loved being part of a big family. I never wanted to go back to Clarice, my Mother, the comedienne after what we called Millie's Summer Camp.

"By the way, I expect you to keep this confidential; you're a counselor, you know."

"It's privileged," she answers in agreement; but I take no satisfaction because I am aware there is really no such thing.

"I can't talk about Fee Lo till I talk about Harry because Fee Lo held me up so I could breathe when Harry up and left me. That's unanimous, now, you know. I don't have a man in my life, who's supposed to be there, that is there.

"But I had Fee Lo and that's why it's so important that you understand exactly the type of friendship that we have because what they're saying is just not possibly true. There is no way Fee Lo could be a killer!"

"For one thing he doesn't have it in him to do such a thing. Maybe he does, but he would not do that to her.

"For another, he loved that woman more than any Mexican that I've ever seen could love a woman; and I say that without a hint of racism. They are not alone but passionate. Mexicans know how to seem to be the most in love people in the world."

" ... But," Dr. Alice says, interrupting and I am stunned. "She might take up with the first person to come along and ask; and he might cut off her face with a machete if she does that or if she says "no!" to him or refuses to let him think he's God and in control and on a daily basis. They will do these things to each other and still profess to be so in love that that's the reason for it. In the name of love they would dismember and kill each other,"

"Is that for real?" I ask my therapist. "Good old country boys are just as bad," I say. "And maybe even Harry the Jerk, who comes from good family!" Harry and I met working for a Senate Investigative Committee. He was general counsel; I was a lowly 2-L still in law school, who carried his briefcase and looked up at him with adoring eyes. I couldn't help myself. He was so attentive. So kind. So complimentary about my intelligence. And different from anything that ever came through my life. Pear-shaped, I admit, but so handsome in his pear-shaped way, the most handsome man I'd ever seen; and it was love at first sight for me, if not for him' as he later claimed. Although I could feel something at the time but looking back, I can accept he just wanted what all those old wrinkled and flaccid bastards on the Committee wanted. There I was, 23, a year late getting through law school due to uncertainty that law was what I wanted to do so it was law school at Georgetown at my Mama's urging because one of her possible-fathers-for-me just happened to teach there and served as a Dean and was able to have the right kind of vote to get me in.

"And I loved every minute of it. I knew immediately that I had made the right choice.

"But you know my favorite Georgetown memory?"

"What?" … I can tell she has not been listening and is not interested in hearing the whole thing and while I wonder just how much I should trust her with, I am desperate at this point, but not that desperate.

"Fee Lo's missing."

"Babe came back on the scene just long enough to drive him crazy and he took that fucking crazy job everybody now says he never showed up for.

"You see, I know he did show up before anybody else conceded. I never told Phyll because she would have killed me for doing it; but I went out there one night when Fee Lo called. I kept them from throwing him off a rack."

I decide not to say anything else to Dr. Alice.

"This is not working," I tell her and pick up my purse. At least I don't have to grab a Kleenex for my eyes and nose. I haven't cried yet.

"Don't leave," she says. "I got distracted by this text. Here look at it! This is what a Mother puts up with daily."

She hands me her I phone and pulls out her Ipad and starts typing. I scroll to the top of the message. Some kid is writing her about having spaghetti for supper. I read it.

"Why should I care about this?" I ask her, handing her back her phone and starting to leave.

She thrusts the Ipad in my face. "Here, you need to sign this first and let me return your card."

I do both, leaving the room and letting the door close silently behind me.

They say we with no children don't have a clue about how children change and dominate your life; but her distraction by a kid's request for spaghetti in the middle of my session seemed a little misplaced, frankly, to me.

I have major work to do and make the immediate decision that the only way I am going to deal with this situation is to do what I would normally have jumped right into. But I have never had a missing best friend before and this feels like real danger to me—not some alleged threat to America taken up by a Senate Committee, which turned out to look more like a partisan escapade. I will go back to my office and start a timeline—a habit formed years ago—and see where it leads this time.

Harry was just a jerk, I can go ahead and tell you that safely now and I no longer love him. Or even like him. But I don't hate him because that would hurt only me.

Yeah.

We were married just two years before he found somebody else. Of course, he was her professor and she was his law student, who promises to be a great lawyer. And, of course, he did not choose her because she was younger and attended the right branch of her Church. Socially speaking. It took me a while to get there and I must admit I would never have made it had Fee Lo, that damned little Mexican, who is my very best friend, not pressed and folded every one of my arguments to the contrary and shot them back at me like paper airplanes.

"You know how you know this?" I demanded at the time. "You're a man and you're all alike!"

He laughed; but I was right. Fee Lo is a heartbreaker too for a lot of other women—till he met Babe that is!

Babe is kinda cute! She is one of those little bitty women, who have brown hair and blue eyes and a helplessness that is so fake any woman within a mile knows it; but no man sees through it. She is an investigative reporter for the *Enterprise* and wanted, above all things between heaven and earth, to earn a Pulitzer Prize for just one story. Not much to ask, right? And she takes chances no ordinary human will take to get there. And now that she is missing, Fee Lo and I both thought they'd find her body someday eaten by crabs and lye and whatever else the bad boys do to little girls they perceive to be in their way. Now he's probably in the same boat and I shudder to think of what they can and will do to Fee Lo if that's how she ended up and he found out about it, which may be why he's missing. Of course, they are saying she is missing because he killed her in an angry rage of jealousy, which I know could not happen ever. I know Fee Lo that well anyway.

I laugh despite the pain growing inside me.

For one thing, if they came after him, it would have been a fight and it would not have been a fair fight with Fee Lo. He has an immense ability to fight low and dirty while it looks like he's doing nothing at all in order to take care of himself. And that is what I am holding onto. And when I find him, if he is still standing, I'm gonna beat the shit out of him myself this time! He will never ever do this to me again.

I throw my purse over my neck and tuck it under my armpit and start his Harley. Fortunately, my legs are long; and I've got a good upper leg grip and sturdy boots that are not for show. Otherwise, I wouldn't drive it. But Phyllis rebelled at the idea I could have her car and Justin, her younger sometimes boyfriend, who is more boy-toy than friend, could take the Harley since we don't have any hope Fee Lo's coming back. Fee Lo also has my car, the wretched wreck again and that is my only car and heaven only knows now where it is. It has its own colorful past; but this time I am not holding out much hope for it. I just hope Fee Lo, bless his soul, has my car to flee in, wherever he is. I may never get it back but the insurance company says I need more evidence than they've been able to get that he's not gonna be able to get it to us!

In other words, I have to give them a dead body to get compensated for my missing car. Makes sense to me. And I didn't bother purchasing insurance to get a rental substitute. A missing friend given the car to use probably won't qualify either when the time comes.

CHAPTER SIXTEEN
Breaking and Entering

"What are you doing?" Phyllis asks as I cover my inside wall by taping an oversized sheet of white paper across it.

"Come on, help me with this," I answer.

She takes her side and pulls the mailing tape out of my side drawer. "So this is our next case, I guess?"

"Don't ask," I answer. "Just think. If you had to say the very first thing that happened, what and when would that be?"

"Fee Lo's call about the crockpot?"

"Not crockpot, the cooking well in his stove. That old Coleman stove in his apartment that's old as God; but has a big cooking pot as the back burner just like his Mama's."

"I remember. Thursday? Friday night?"

I thumbed through the calendar. "Let's do this right," I say. "I'll talk on the way. Can you get it down?"

"Can I get it down?" she says with a disgusted note in her voice.

She hands me the keys to her car:

"You don't want to ride piggy-back on the Harley?" I ask with a grin.

"F-ing no," she says, slamming the passenger door. "You told me he called you about ten."

"It was Friday. He'd gone over the causeway to go to HEB to get the stuff on his Mother's list."

"To cook beans?"

"To cook her beans the way she cooks them but for Babe. That got him to the pot. He opened the lid and Babe—or somebody—had put the papers in there. It was her investigation and on top of it was a letter, handwritten by her, giving him instructions to copy them and put them some place safe. He called in tears and I went running over. We took care of the papers that night and we both read them but I didn't pay as much attention as I should have. Couldn't, actually, it was above my pay grade all the way. Chemical formulas. Emails. Texts. One short, to-the-point letter that left nothing to doubt. Major working scientist threatened to leave immediately if the project didn't stop. He left, Babe scribbled on her notes, and she was on his trail. I thought she was up to something rather than on to something and just stringing Fee Lo along again like the little rubber duckie he becomes in her presence. I didn't know what was going to happen."

"Now, I've seen those papers twice. I don't have Babe's papers and I don't know where Fee Lo hid them." I tell Phyllis:

"Remind me to ask Sharon Donaldson about the identity of that scientist. No, better still, get that list she gave us of employees at East Field. Let's see if anybody on it sounds like a doctor. Why didn't I think to ask where to find him when she was spilling the beans to us?"

"I doubt she even knows who the scientists out there are," Phyll says; but I know she is trying to make me feel better.

I went over the list and Phyll typed them into the computer for a Google check.

What did you come up with?" I ask. We've been too busy to talk before.

"I don't know who it is," Phyllis answers, "But there are two of them, both chemists. Lars Andersen, Phd., University of Edinburgh, long list of crap he's done. And David Dickerson, Phd., The University of Texas. Not as much science info as Andersen, but still a long listing of things he's done and written about" As efficient as ever, Phyll digs a list out of her notebook, spreads them out.

"I'll start tracking down their whereabouts tomorrow. It's too late tonight. And we might even ask Sharon Rose what she knows about the two of them and other Departments before they worked in East Field."

"Okay," I say, "I feel the need for movement. Let's check out Fee Lo's place and see if it looks like he's been hiding out there. Not many people know where he lives. He gave us his key right? We think he's in trouble, right? He would want us to use that key to find him, right?"

"I'm thinking," she says, "because I think you're thinking we would violate the law by breaking and entering."

"Just in case our theory is not interpreted as we do," I say. "I'm just not ready to give up my law license just yet," I say.

I hear Phyll 's "humph" of breath and would not be able to count all the times she's gained entrance to a place she needed to go using the same kind of rationale.

"What you're talking about is not illegal," she says like an expert rendering an opinion based on solid law. "We are the only two friends he has in this world who would court danger to make sure he's not in danger. We can defend our need and duty to rescue him!"

She's as serious as a heart attack and I decide he's the only one who could complain; and he won't for sure.

We are both quiet as we walk up four flights of stairs to Fee Lo's loft. I have seen it once since he moved in and was impressed by its minimalism. He has three or four pieces of furniture for the essentials and no extra do-dads.

I put my key in the lock and Phyllis and I both pick ourselves off the floor of the hallway where we land.

"What the F happened?" Phyllis asks, dusting off her new Lemon Yellow, or some such, black leggings, which are now covered with a fine dusting of something that looks like flour. "That f-ing, Fee Lo, is this his idea of a joke?"

"Probably," I say, rubbing the elbow I'd fallen on. "That hurts!" I come close to whining.

"It should," she says, testing the knob on the door, which is now an empty hole. She pushes her fingers in and grabs against the door, pulling. "I've never seen anything like that," she says.

"You feelin' alright?" I ask. "No dizziness? Thirst? Pain any place except your pride?"

"Mad," Phyllis answers, pulling and then pushing the door, which swings into the room. "These leggings cost a hundred dollars." She gasps! "Is Fee Lo this bad?"

"No," I answer. The room is a man-made wreck: "Somebody obviously is as curious as we are and looks to have been in a big hurry."

I take out my I-phone and photograph the missing knob and take a series of pictures of the room at large. A genuine loft, it huddles in the corner of the width of the building, two sets of oversized windows with exterior arched concrete frames embrace the building. One pane is stretched and another is open. I look out without touching. A clear ledge wraps around the entire floor.

"Look at this," I tell Phyll. Do you think Fee Lo could have escaped that way?"

"This whole thing is more sophisticated than you would anticipate from him," she says.

Fee Lo has the top floor of the rundown building that has recently been turned into high-end lofts.

"His Dad died and he used the inheritance to buy it. The payments and fees are higher than rent, so he struggles. But it probably is a good investment if he can keep it."

"Take a look at this," she says. The old hand-blown glass in the oversized window is bent more than broken. Some object caved it outward. I get close enough to photograph the point of impact.

"Obviously, he was here when they came looking," I say. "Look for hair—it is so patently a head print." I do so and turn away. "Is it what I think?" Phyllis asks, crossing both arms over her ample chest.

"I don't know," I say, taking a series of pictures, trying to get as close as I can. Fee Lo can take care of himself in a fight. But it looks wiped clean anyway, which would suggest that he didn't take the time to do it, but that somebody did.

"See if he has Ziplocks," I say. "We will put some of this powder in it," I tell Phyllis, who is taking in Fee Lo's interesting digs like a prospective buyer.

I photograph the immediate area. Standing against the opposite wall I try to take in the room to see if I can detect a path or pattern for the action, or any other clues.It is all one room. The bright red, chrome trimmed Coleman Stove, a real wood burner turned gas, stands along one wall. The table between it and the room looks untouched. I photograph the surface. Garlic peeled and crushed, drying. A small amount of oil congealed in the skillet. Beans in a basket, drained for days now, a dried salt ring evident on the table. Roasted salt pork, cooked so dry it looks like tiny pieces of thick, dried leather. Cilantro, wilted and turning brown. Water in the cooking pot. Full. Cold. I dip a finger in it. Touch it, feel grease and photograph it. Leave the lid lying off.

"I thought suburbanism would be different from the big city," I say.

Because I interrupt our intentional silence, Phyllis jumps. Turning toward her, I see tears running down Phyllis' face and feel my own

eyes well up. "Let's don't do that," I bark. "If I start I may not stop!"
It is the most honest disclosure I'd ever made to my assistant, who
looks up startled.

"How long has it been?" she asks suspiciously, turning her head
and squinting her eyes.

"Ten or fifteen years. Maybe longer. You know. Same time since
I had sex."

We both laugh.

"Wow! You had me going for a minute. I don't guess I should
offer to vacuum this mess up."

"Who can we call to help us?" I ask her. "I don't have a clue who
did this. It could have been the cops. Or Rutter? Who knows? I just
don't want to tip too many people off yet. Have we left any footprints
in that white powder?"

"We can smush 'em."

"We can smush 'em all the way out the way we came in. We've
got enough pictures."

Every drawer is open. Pulled out and away. Contents on the floor.
Closet open. Nothing left hanging. No doors going anywhere. Covers
off the bed. Let's check the bathroom and get out of here."

I look again into the deep cooking well.

"Why did Fee Lo fill up that pot when he left everything else out
to die?" I ask her. Or did somebody else do it to throw us off. I try to
think about what he said his Mama told him but it was just not coming.

Doing as much damage control as possible, we slip back across
the room, I first, stepping into my earlier prints and Phyllis mushing
them out with her boxy pumps. We locate the doorknob and push it
into the hole after wiping it on my tee-shirt. Then we go down the
four sets of stairs as hurriedly and quietly as we can, which is no
small feat for two women who don't exercise as much as we should
or could.

CHAPTER SEVENTEEN
Timeline Two

"We know we are not sure about this first entry," I say, going back to the timeline. Can you go dump the pictures and print anything that comes out?"

"Sure," she says and takes the phone and the camera and starts to the storage room. "But we need to come up with some Code."

"Gotcha."

"Next we have to deal with the Rutter Job. I know he went there. I know he was there. That was Wednesday, before that Friday and it was at least 2 a.m. in the morning, not afternoon." She gives me a stern look.

"You went there by yourself?" she asks.

"He called me in a panic. 'Don't ask questions,' he said. 'Bring the Harley and make as much noise as you can. Stay away from the gate. The fence is cut and open on 8 Mile Road. Come to the second stack and rev the engine. Say something but call me Sweetie and tell me I promised you tonight would be different. It will be.' And he hung up the phone and I threw on jeans and boots and a hard hat for some reason because the last time I was out there when he called, something big came flying off that rack. This time it is Fee Lo, who slides down a rope from the top, jumps on the Harley and drives from behind with his arms around me. We cut out faster than I've ever gone on a motorcycle."

Phyll is stunned.

"I don't believe you are that stupid," she says.

"Well I was," I concede. "Impulsive too. I thought somebody shot at us; but he said it was my imagination. He just wanted the night off, he said. Had a hot date later and planned to dump me. And that's all he ever told me. But I know something big and heavy went off that stack the time before. And he said, 'that's how it happens.' But he never explained what. Said it was better if I didn't know things I was too much of a girl to hear."

I add another entry. "I went out there after court and ended up seeing Sharon Donaldson, Director of Human Relations, she denied she had ever seen Fee Lo in the most credible voice I've ever heard; said that Fee Lo was never hired at Rutter, never worked at Rutter, and that he had never been there to her knowledge; and that she would know because she alone does all the hiring and firing for that unit. Every new employee of any stripe goes through her initial examination."

"Wow!" Phyll says.

"I insisted that I had taken him to work and dropped him off; but she said I was wrong and if Jack McNelly listened to all her calls, as she said, he knows that I have been out there at least twice now."

I am beginning to think our timing is off and that too much happened too fast to keep the timeline straight.

"Add those two times to the timeline," she says. "Our timing might be way off, but we need not to forget the events. That first call he made was at least a month before the second. The first time I thought nothing of it. Just another Fee Lo escapade and he laughed about it and my concern.

"But then by the second time, everything had gone South because Sharon Donaldson came clean and admitted she hired him and that she sent him to the East Field to find out for her what was going on and he disappeared!

"In fact," Phyll said. "She said he was trespassing if he was out there helping Babe."

"I stopped arguing with her because I knew it was likely that he was helping Babe. "

"But then she told us," Phyll says and makes a notation on the third entry that he was there and disappeared. "After that," Phyll says. "Nobody knew where he was, and no one has seen him since."

"And that was our Sharon Donaldson," Phyllis says. "I'll put her first here, denying she knows Fee Lo; then way over here I'm gonna add her mom as my patient, which will be our code for what she told us. I went back to see her Mom yesterday. She knows more than Sharon thinks," Phyll says. "She said she's seen this guy on their street. Sounds like what I think McNelly looks like. He comes by when she's on the porch and waves."

"You think the two of us together can remember all this?" Phyllis asks if I just put key words, like Mom, patient?"

"Unless we drink three margaritas," I say. "I'm good for two. The third one is always a killer."

"Gotcha. I'll put it on my hand and hide it in the safe."

"Not a good idea. I don't want anybody chopping your hand off to get our code."

Phyllis gasped and hid her hand between her boobs. I started laughing and then couldn't stop.

"If you knew how funny that looks."

"Sorry, it feels very real. And dangerous. What do we do next?" She acts as if she is running out of patience.

"I'm thinking. Have we worked with anybody you had a good impression of at the PD that you remember?"

"You know me, I generally like all lawmen and I think they get a bum deal. But I don't know who to think about because I don't know what we're gonna need."

"We need to find out if there is a report on Fee Lo's break-in and if anybody reported Babe missing. What does her newspaper say? Do you remember her given name?"

"Something like her Mama," Phyllis says.

"She used to call fairly frequently to see if we had heard from Fee Lo any time she couldn't find him. Look through the books and see if she gave us a number. Would we have a carbon of her message?"

Phyll nods.'

"Try the two weeks he was in the Valley…".

Phyllis went to the storage closet and dragged open a large drawer.

That will keep her busy for a while, I am thinking. And although I did not anticipate success at all, Phyllis calls out: You were right, it's like the Mama, Laverne, but with an a ending, Lorena Burnett, and she left me a number for him. Two in fact. One is her cell for sure. I'll bet the other one is the *Enterprise*."

Prancing back into the room, she is shoeless now with hips wagging and already typing numbers into one of her throw downs.

"On the day he left, she called and said he had his cell phone off," Phyllis says, reading the yellow carbon of the call note. "Called at ten that morning. Said if we heard from him to have him call. Said it was not urgent."

Phyllis re-checked the call pad, "No, that was six months ago?"

"Can't be," I say.

"Can't be, but it is," Phyllis turns the other sheets. "Called three days later asking if we'd heard anything. Didn't ask him to call. Said he'd call when he felt like it. You think he broke up with her?"

"Not a chance in Hell," I answer. "She had him so whipped nothing could have come between them after she came back helpless. Where was he then?"

"That was still during the Dickless Mess. He had been fired and should have been in the Laredo area about then. He wasn't at Rutter until at least four weeks after he got back from Laredo and ya'll did your do-sey-do with Judge Raleigh. By the way I agree with you, he's so cute. Think he's gonna go crazy like the last Judge?"

"Hope not," I say, "that will prove that my man-picker is really messed up if he does. He's young so he should be more mature than those older guys. The middle-aged group in the Sixties guys are a lost generation."

"So he wasn't at Rutter yet; but we know he was here when I went out to pick him up on the Harley. And, we now know he was hired at Rutter and probably was there by then. He's not the kind to sit and wait for a job to find him."

"But this one did," Phyllis says. "This one has Babe written all over it.

"Which is all strange; but if he worked there that might have let her move on," Phyll muses.

"He worked there, Phyll, and now we know it was in East Field and the key to what we are looking for is happening out there, right under our noses."

Settling into my extravagantly expensive soft red leather executive desk chair, a gift from my Mother to give me courage, I lean back and put my bare feet on the corner of my desk, which would send my Mother up the frigging wall if she saw it. She's one of life's funniest women but she's a tight ass without a dab of humor where I am concerned. She still thinks I haven't accomplished enough because I'm not a famous lawyer yet.

Nervous, I get up to pace and walk over, put the last date Phyll found on the board, which requires me to go back six months, and insert a scribbled note between two others. Was it going on that early? I cannot remember when he went out there for the first time. I settle back again, re-lift my feet and remember another date.

"If you're gonna pace, I'm going to get your files ready for tomorrow.

I've got to go home sometime tonight. I started."

"Shower here. You say the couch sleeps good. I don't want to be here alone and I don't want to take the long drive to the West End on the Harley. Put the files together anyway. Just tell me what time to be where. Don't suppose you'd let me use your car…".

"Meet me here," Phyllis answers after giving it serious thought. "But if you disappear on me and leave me with Justin and that motorcycle, I'm quitting for good. That's all I've got to say about that."

I laugh. "Driving the Harley's not so bad. I get lots of propositions. Much more than normal since normal is none."

"I don't need that. I have an oversexed young bird at home. At least when he lights for a day or two."

"That's what you get for robbing the cradle," I say.

She closes the door and I lean back in my chair again and close my eyes. Something at Fee Lo's place is out of order.

Something major that we missed.

I go through pictures on my I-phone and put them on the computer and start making prints. I have a new printer that spits them out like magic and I pull them off as each one comes out, searching but finding nothing. I slip them into my desk drawer rather than adding them to the wall. Too many, I am thinking. Maybe one at a time will bring it back. But I exhaust my examination of several in turn and it doesn't.

Phyllis knocks and comes back into the room with a list and a stack of files, opens the briefcase, and puts them in, closing it.

"Let me see those," she says. "Something sure ain't right; but I can't put my finger on it."

"Great minds," I say. "I have the feeling he was there when all that happened and left us a clue he had to act fast on and that we have failed to pick up on." We each take a stack of photographs and spread them out across the desk.

"I don't want to go back," she says. "I'm afraid we would be pressing our luck a second time without an officer we can trust to wait and see who brings it up besides us."

"I know what you mean," I agree.

"I'm thinking about that. Tell me something: What was the last conversation you had with Fee Lo?" Phyll asks.

"He took my car. Said those were his tires on it. Which they were in part; he rotated them after he drove it to the Valley. Left his keys.

Threw them on the desk. I complained because it was a big chunk, which clanged around on the bike."

"I heard that conversation. You told him to take everything off; but the bike key, and he said he wasn't going to be needing them and had no place to put 'em anyway. You said something appropriate like: 'Damn you, Fee Lo! You are always too much trouble!'

"'Thinking ahead, I remember he said that he has to hit you with a sledge hammer sometimes!'"

"That Son of a bitch," I say and pick up the keys. "He never expected to need these again. Tell me what these go to, if you can." I go back to the photographs, examining each with a plastic hand-held sheet that enlarges the original. I go through nine or ten, finding nothing before Phyllis comes back.

"You're not going to be happy about this," Phyllis says, coming into the room with a page she has printed from the Internet on types of keys. This is the Harley. This is his loft. This is a bank deposit box or my name's not Phyllis. This is a post office box. Local. It looks just like mine. This is something I don't recognize; but could be a locker key or a trunk key. It looks cheap enough to be for one of those painted cardboard deals you took to college. This looks like another house key. So does this, but older and worn—I'm guessing this one's his mother's."

"You have her number?"

"Only if he called us while he was in the Valley from her phone, which is unlikely since he has a cell."

"You know her name?"

"Can I guess Mrs. Hernandez? He said they were good Catholics. Never mentioned another guy after his Dad died."

"How many you think there are?"

"Hernandezes? Probably about 50 percent of the Chicanos, which in the Valley can be 90 percent of the population."

"You think the other's Lorena's?"

"I don't know," she says with resignation. "He had so many women; but I do have Babe's address if you'd like to drive by and see if maybe her place looks like his."

"Should we take an officer?" Phyllis asks.

"What do we have to lose?" I ask, much to my regret later.

CHAPTER EIGHTEEN
Sharon Takes Another Look

"That woman came by again," Sharon writes.

"No emails," came the quick reply.

Silence.

She picks up the phone.

"Sorry, I wasn't thinking."

"That's dangerous."

"Understand. She is not taking no for an answer."

"I'll send somebody to have a little talk with her."

"Are you sure you are doing the right thing on this?"

"No choice at this point. We just need a couple more weeks now."

"I still don't understand," Sharon says.

"You're not supposed to understand; you're supposed to do your job."

"But...".

"No butts about it, when your employer tells you that an operation is privileged and confidential for your employer, remember? You keep your mouth shut."

Sharon hangs up the phone, scans through her emails and deletes the last one. In the bottom of her desk drawer, Felipe's file lurks like a dagger about to spring. She had been told to ditch it; but something holds her back.

It is difficult, Sharon thinks, for a Christian to lie this way. Now the file has taken on a presence of its own. She almost fears opening the drawer in the event some camera has been installed to judge what she does and says.

Tonight, perhaps. After dark. Maybe she can take it with her then if she works late enough. Meanwhile, Sharon thinks, put on a happy face, Sharon Rose.

"Hello," Sharon says pertly into the phone. "Is this Martha Calhoun?"

"No but I'll get her. This is her Mother."

"Hi, Mrs. Calhoun?"

"No, Lawrence, Mr. Calhoun died."

"Oh, I'm so sorry about that. This is Sharon Donaldson from Rutter. I wanted to set up a meeting with Martha. Is it a bad time?"

"No harm, Honey, Martha's father died a long, long time ago. She's coming down the stairs right this minute."

"Hi," the voice matches Sharon's in false perkiness.

"Martha, hi, this is Sharon Donaldson at Rutter. We want you to come in for an interview."

"Oh, that is so exciting!"

"I know. Rutter is an exciting place to work. Come get to know our family. Can you make it today?"

"I could, but late."

"How late?" Sharon asks, seeing her opening. "We actually close at five but if you could make it a few minutes before, I'll just wait for you. I read your application and you sound like somebody we need."

"I'll leave my job a little early and be there by 4:30. My boss is very supportive and thinks this is something I ought to do. He thinks I'm smart."

"I can tell that's true," Sharon says. "Your papers are very impressive. Good grades. Good reference letters. A great statement of mission and purpose. See you at 4:30, my dear."

Sharon hangs up the phone, not looking at her desk drawer and determines not to do so for the remainder of the day.

"Hello, I am looking for Jonathan Kenyon."

Silence. Smiles in case there are cameras.

"Oh, wonderful. Mr. Kenyon, this is Sharon Donaldson at Rutter and I want to invite you to come out to Rutter for an interview. I have your application and it's just wonderful." Smile. Relax. Three more to call. This can be a busy day.

CHAPTER NINETEEN
Breaking and entering \ Times Two

"Do you think we're in the process of becoming habitual criminals?"

"No, I think we're feeling desperate," I tell my legal assistant and accomplice in crime. "Rand said he would cover for us. Right?"

"Yeah, but I fear he wants my body and I don't think I'm going to be delivering on any schedule that can keep him on a string."

"Hope springs eternal," I say. "Don't give him the come on just for me, it's your decision." Our voices are creaking. "Are you that scared?"

"Yes. In a word. Scared? No. Terrified. I don't like the way that guy sounds on the phone."

"Pay him no mind. He's a coward or he would have come in person and roughed us up a little bit."

"Are you kidding me?"

"Yes. He's a douche bag. He scared me too. I just don't admit to such things."

"Was he serious?"

"How do I know if he's serious? I don't know him. Hell, I don't know Rutter for that matter, but apparently a lot of people do. What are they doing out there that causes them to have a security force larger than their work force?"

"Something for the government, maybe? The military? Poison gas."

"Chemicals that kill instantly?"

"Special killing devices they're shipping to third world dictators?" We both start laughing.

"You know, we're just a couple of ditsy females looking for a man who drops out of sight on us all the time and gets into more trouble than ten boyfriends," I say.

"And drives a Harley and sticks us with it when he takes off on another episode."

"Why are we so concerned?"

"Beats me," I answer. "Not one of these f-ing keys fits this door." We are at the back door of Babe's little cottage, a small, white concrete block box with all shutters—literally the ancient kind that look like blinds turned wrong-side out as storm shutters—and closed as tight as the proverbial drum.

"Here, let me try," Phyl whispers now that we have gone beyond the conspiracy preparation stage and have taken the first step toward committing what we both fully understand can be viewed as an intentional crime by some opponent some day—burglary of a dwelling. Since it is at night, the law allows the state to argue that we could be presumed to be sex maniacs breaking in to sexually assault someone.

Poor guy.

Of course, we think its explainable since both of them are missing and would want us to do what we are doing to find them, which includes checking this place out.

Phyllis takes the key she had previously identified as Babe's and puts it in the lock and it turns immediately. The door swings in slightly and hits up against an object that slides slowly only when we both push hard on the door. It takes pretty significant force but when we are both inside and have closed the door, I turn on the light in my IPhone and both of us scream bloody murder, looking down as we are, on the ultra-white face of what appears to be a male corpse wearing a policeman's uniform.

"Oh my Gawd," Phyllis drawls. "It's Rand!"

"Rand?" I ask.

"Rand." She answers and holds her breath.

Instinctively, I touch his neck and find a faint pulse. I don't go around finding corpses that often; but I had a client once who fainted all the time. In court. In the office. The only way I could tell if she was still alive was checking her pulse points.

"Let's get the hell out of here," Phyllis screams. "I've seen everything I need to see."

"No, we can't do that. He's still alive. We've got to get him out of here." I put an arm under his shoulders and lift him up. He starts to move, moaning.

"What was that?" he asks, letting me pull him into a sitting position.

"Help me," I tell him. "We've got to get you out of here. Whoever put that knot on your head might come back with a bigger weapon if he saw your uniform."

Phyllis is already moving toward the door.

"Don't touch anything," I command, shining the light on my IPhone around the room until I have satisfied myself we are alone. Following the light around the room, I ask: "Notice something different?"

I can see the whites of Phyllis' eyes in the dark: "I can't notice. I can't think."

"Try not to. Just look."

"The place is spotless?"

"Not a hair out of place. Just like Babe to be a perfect little housekeeper. I'll bet she dusted before she would let them carry her off."

I cover the doorknob with the bottom of my shirt, wipe it and open the door slowly. We repeat the same backward escape we had done earlier at Fee Lo's; but this time we hold up the weak officer, who feels like he is twice our size. When we reach the car, we shove the groggy officer into the backseat and put the car in neutral and roll it out of the driveway before turning on the engine. The lights come on automatically and by this time Rand has recovered enough to look around.

"My car's gone," he says. All three of us look around, sitting low in the seats as we drive out of the peaceful, moderate-income area that seems dark and closed up for the night.

"Now I'm scared," I say. "I think Rand got the greeting we were supposed to have gotten."

"What do we do now?" Phyllis asks.

"First thing, when we get far enough away you're gonna take that throw down phone you keep in your purse so Jason won't find it, and you're going to report a body."

"To whom?"

"To the Galveston police," I answer, "that's what we would do if we had thought Rand was dead and left him and made our getaway. Since they are waiting for us, they would have known we would come looking for Rand. The whole thing must have really upset their apple cart if they took off themselves ahead of our arrival."

I am already thinking about where the three of us can spend the night without pacing the floor all night. Decided there is no place and elect to go the office and prepare a brief.

"Write a brief?" Phyllis exclaims. "How the hell can you think about writing a f-ing brief? At a time like this?"

"We've got to be very busy and very much on a schedule. We have fallen into something bigger than we can handle even with Rand here's help. I need to think."

Once inside the office, we walk together to check every room and tighten every window lock. When we are sure no one is inside with us, I lower all of the outside storm shutters and turn on all the lights. "Bring me a file, any file that has a brief or Motion due on it." I tell my assistant. "And bring me a stack of books. Turn on your computer and do a Google Search on any topic you think might be related and bring me that subpoena that federal agent served on Fee Lo when Dickless Little took him to federal court on the civil rights suit. You can find his number in that file."

"Is there a method to this madness?" Phyl asks, going through the motions as she asks.

"Thinking on the fly. I want us to appear to be busy and working late if anybody just happens to drive by. I want the computer to support what we say. I want actual work going on to support what we say; but also to calm us down. We don't know what Rand might have said to somebody to give himself an excuse to go over there. But, just in case, we need to be busy on something real."

"Why do you need the fed file on Fee Lo?"

"I'm really looking for that guy, the one you met in Dallas. He reminded me about cross-examining him on another case; but I am sure he served the subpoena when Dickless removed his case against Fee Lo to federal court. And you met him in Dallas with Roger Shutte. I know the feds know what is happening. I want to find out why this guy's always within six degrees of separation from me all the time and see if he can help us. But, I need to think about that before I act on it."

"Rand did you by any chance have your service revolver?"

He searches his gun belt.

"I think I did. I don't know now but it's sure not here." Ordinarily calm and collected, Rand is still a little spacey.

"I'm just a little old helper here," Phyllis whines. "Tell me what to stir and I'll keep it going. You think. And think. It's okay with me if we just lie down right here on the floor and hide under the desks all night."

"We might do that too before it's over," I say. "I wish to God I knew whether the PD went to Babe's."

"I can tell them Rand looked pretty dead to me, which was why I called."

"You never know," I say. "But don't let that be wishful thinking. These people are crazy. And evil."

Rand returns from the restroom, where he obviously doused his head in the sink. His hair is wet and dripping and his cheeks are red. He looks at Phyllis: "I told myself you'd be nothing but trouble," he says. "My psychic antennae were going crazy all over the place. But this shit was not on my mind. What are ya'll messed up in anyway?"

"How's your head?" I ask, partly from concern but also to stall his questions.

"Do you have any idea what happened?"

"I got a key from the evidence locker and went there to make sure the two of you would be able to do what you needed, but I didn't feel right about knowing what you were going to do without covering your back. Too many things go wrong around here all the time."

"You're right about that," I say. "You brought us luck. I'm sorry you took the brunt of it. Any idea what happened?"

"He was serious, whatever and whoever he was, and he is big. Hit me like a ton of bricks. I swear he had a blackjack. I feel tazed now that I've come around."

"Any idea who it was?"

"No, but he is big," Rand repeats. "I'd guess he's right handed. Muscular. He's done this before because he knew just where to hit. If he'd gotten one of you, I'm not sure you'd still be here."

"How did he know?" I ask.

"Beats me," Rand says innocently. "I didn't even tell my partner where I was going or what was up."

"Did you talk to anybody over the phone?"

"Just Phyll."

"That's not good," I say, looking around the office. "Phyll did you use your cell phone or the landline?"

"The landline."

"Well, we won't use it again except on purpose. You have that pre-paid handy?"

Phyllis hands it over, but blushes when Rand smiles.

"I knew you'd be trouble," he repeats.

"Don't go drawing any conclusions that might happen to be wrong," Phyllis tells him. "You don't have any idea; but this woman I work for is the trouble; she draws trouble like a magnet!"

At this all three of us laugh.

"You're cute when you're embarrassed," Rand says. "Can you make a cup of coffee when you're under fire like this?"

"That I can do," Phyll says. "Without thinking."

When the two of them leave for the kitchen, I dial the number at the bottom of the service papers in Fee Lo's federal case.

"You may not remember me," I say when he answers and blush when he says: "Oh, I do. I wondered if you might ever give me a call. I even remember that voice. I remember that you are somewhere close to six feet tall. You have nice red hair, honey-darkened red, not from a bottle, I'm betting. And if I recall correctly, after seeing you sashay from the room in Dallas, he was right when he told me to look for a hot woman with the best ass."

"Wow! You are Mr. Eye Witness Personified, aren't you?" I say, laughing, and enjoying the moment. My memory is good. The name on here is different but he's the same one. "I am sitting here working late and it just got boring. I don't suppose you're bored too."

I smile when I hang up the phone.

You're a low-life bitch, I say to myself. Led that poor sucker along so easily, you ought to be ashamed.

"Wow!" he says when he gets here and realizes it is more than a two-person party. "If I told you this was the first time I've ever been so easily reeled-in, you'd believe me; wouldn't you?"

"Sure," I answer and give him a good-natured hug. "I do this every night. But tonight I need somebody with special expertise to talk to and I think you're it!"

CHAPTER TWENTY
Sharon Rose Discovers a Problem

Jonathan Kenyon sits across from Sharon Rose Donaldson and she briefly thinks how nice it would be to be young and ambitious and talented all over again. He is a talker though and she lets him fill the room with his optimism and plans for the future. His youth, enthusiasm, faith in everything, and healthy good looks are the best thing that has happened to her since that deputy came into her life and rekindled all her youthful hope of living happily forever after some day with someone. Something inside her makes her want to scream at him to get out and run as far away from Rutter Industries as he can get; but she doesn't.

Sharon Rose smiles.

And while she is smiling, she reaches down to the left side of her desk and pulls out the drawer containing that Deputy's file.

It is as empty as the day they wheeled in this new rosewood desk and announced her promotion to Director of Human Relations. Carefully, she closes the drawer!

Well, she thinks and wonders how quickly after her email and his call had he searched her office and found the file. Or had he known all along? And would she be finding a pink slip on her desk now that he had seen her go for the file on his camera system? He would know that she had copied the deputy's file. And he would know that Felipe Hernandez not only had been hired at Rutter, he was in security; and he is as missing as a soul can be.

No one, nowhere, knows where Felipe Hernandez has gone.

And the panic goes higher than Sharon Rose Donaldson and the man, who torments her every day with his pompous pronouncements of what she will and will not do and what she will and will not say.

"I would swear I had a box of Kleenex in that drawer," she says, loud enough for any taping system. "Excuse me please for just a moment." She steps into her private restroom and pulls off enough toilet tissue to blow her nose. Does so. Flushes it, washes her hands and returns to her office. She holds out her hand to the young man. "Congratulations! This is a perfect day to introduce you to everyone so that you can see the Rutter Family firsthand. You're also perfect for us; let's see if we seem like a good fit to you."

She guides the young man from her office, eyes focused on the door; her thoughts focused on the future.

CHAPTER TWENTY-ONE
The Timeline Grows

After Court I go by the Police Department and get what Phyll ordered and asked me to pick up: copies of Babe's police report and a new copy of one on Fee Lo. Apparently, the folks at Rutter are asking for help finding them.

"They say he got away from there with important intellectual property information that he shouldn't have had access to in the first place," Jake, the FBI Investigator says. "I think we know what that is, but it didn't come from him. I know he's your friend and hope he wasn't that close; but apparently, he used his charm on a young woman there, Sharon Rose Donaldson. . .". Jake shrugs as if embarrassed for me.

"Who is the same one you agreed to protect. Did that not happen?" He doesn't answer.

"I met her," I interrupt. "She first said he never worked there but after McNelly attacked her, she sought us out and told us another story. She warned us that McNelly was also claiming that Fee Lo had stolen important papers from Rutter. She gave us the documents that we took to Schutte. Does any of this come back to you."

"I actually never got it," he says. "I had to turn it over to my captain, who has a special group for that. And now they have turned Fee Lo in as missing in action and urge that he took intellectual property from Rutter," he says. "They are bringing charges against him."

"I should tell you now," I tell the agent, who just happens to have my favorite name, Jake. "The documents I took to Shutte came from her. And she told us she hired Fee Lo and she also told us she asked him to check out East Field and find out what was going on out there for her. Maybe she decided to do her own investigation."

He seems to absorb this silently.

"Let me try to check on something," Rand suggests, and leaves the room with another of Phyl's throw down phones. "This is not the phone you called in the report on, is it?" he asks her.

"No," she answers.

"Joe, this is Rand. Was there a strange call to that reporter woman's house last night? I was in the neighborhood and saw a commotion. I almost stopped. But I was onto something hot."

Long silence as he listens.

"Really?" Rand asks. *(Long Pause)* "You don't mean it!""You don't mean it!" he says and hangs up the phone.

Rand turns back to Shadow. "If you get a call, I'm not here, or I just got here five minutes ago, whatever you have to say. There was a body at Babe's house when we were there. Her editor is coming over before they move it—apparently it is still fresh and forensics is going crazy. They may have found half of the Babe and Fee Lo team."

"So that's why…," I start and then I stop.

"Maybe Sharon Donaldson's nervousness was from knowing something had or was about to happen to Babe. I had been certain from her demeanor and her off -the-wall-hint when she called the second time that Fee Lo, if he had been there, might be more involved than I thought. 'If I hoped to find Babe alive,' she told me by phone, 'I might want to find her before Fee Lo did.'

"And why? I had asked her and Donaldson hinted, Babe had something going on with somebody that Fee Lo didn't care for at Rutter!"

"Oh, no!" Phyll says

"If I had only known to ask the right questions," I say, "we might have more information than we do now."

"You might want to look through these two missing persons reports," Jake says. "Rutter's the one that filed them; but both are signed by Sharon Rose Donaldson as the head of Human Resources. Maybe it's worth talking to her again," Jake suggests.

"Who is this contact person?" I ask.

"Jack McNelly," Rand answers. "Why does that sound familiar to me?"

"Beats me, I say. "Sounds pretty Texas-ee though."

I am beginning to wonder just how much this Jake, the Federal Agent, who is tall and good looking and all those things I require in a man, has between his ears, when he makes his second remark of the evening.

"He's a Texas Ranger, I think. Not one but a couple of them put together. But both have been dead for several decades now."

"That doesn't pass the smell test," Phyll says. "We could go break and enter and find out exactly who he is," she adds in obvious jest.

"Like that got us real far the last time," I say.

"Well, it certainly helps me out," Rand concludes while the federal agent shakes his head.

"If you people are habituals," he suggests. "I don't think I can hang with you."

Phyllis comes in with another hot cup of coffee and hands it to Rand. "Try this one and see if it tastes more like coffee now that you've been sitting up awhile. I'm not really an expert on concussions, so I don't know exactly what's best. You tell me. Does it feel better to sit up or do you want to lie down again. There's a couch in the waiting room that's pretty comfortable. I know because when she works all night, I do too. There's also a shower back there behind her office if you think that would help."

"This is good," Rand says weakly, obviously enjoying the attention.

"Do you feel safe enough with me to go for a walk?" Jake asks me.

"Are you packing?" I ask.

"Not where you can see, Ma'am."

CHAPTER TWENTY-TWO
Duty Calls

Phyllis does the Courthouse run while I make a trip back to Dallas with Jake, the tall, lanky lawman. Hard duty I've taken on, I know you are thinking; and I confess, I am intrigued.

He tells me very little except that he has visited with Sharon Donaldson and her Mother and they are doing fine. His boss has someone on them, he said, and I can relax. I don't ask, but I decide that maybe this is the guy who bicycles by each day. Then he does something that surprises me. He says nothing else at all. He is a man of few words and Dallas is four hours away and the ride is not particularly exciting in a blue nondescript vehicle that is not luxurious. Apparently, he has no budget for flying although I let him know I would pay for my own ticket.

I'm glad Phyllis loaded me down with files. I read them thoroughly and ask permission to make some calls and I get a few of them worked out.

"So that's how it's done," he says with a grin after I do my usual with Edward Stephens.

I ignore him and go into another file.

Finally, he reaches out a hand and takes my wrist and then opens my palm and locks my hand in his. It's the most exotic advance that I've ever felt. I say noting. He says nothing. We sit like that for several miles until his phone rings.

He lets it go to message. Then it comes back incessantly again and again until he picks up.

"Sorry," he says into the phone. "Checking a tire."

He listens, then says: "Sure, But I have a problem with that."

He waits through another tirade.

"You gave me a job. I'll do it. You'll get everything I get."

He hangs up the phone.

I lower a window to let the wind in and put it back up to physically release the tension.

"Thanks," he said. "I don't know how he does it but that was my boss. I am not my own man and he wants to make sure I know that every day of my life."

"You could do something else," I offer.

"I could. You are right. I could. But this one's personal now."

"Why?"

"Just personal by this time," he says and turns the car radio on to NPR, over which we both listen to a program of emotional stories. It is a bad fit. I feel that an important moment was lost and resent it for some reason.

We were coming into South Dallas and made the connection from 45 to 75 and then 20 and into an area that skirts the city on the Southwest side. I had been there before but it was by Uber and I really didn't watch the route. He maneuvers around traffic like it is an old friend he's going to see and he enjoys the duty.

When we get to Roger Shutte's building, he pulls the car into a slot that is open and marked "visitor" around the perimeter walkway, and we get out.

"May I leave my things?"

"I wouldn't," he says. "I can lock it but the case looks inviting."

I throw it over my shoulder and he takes it off and puts it over his own.

"I've never had a man willing to carry my purse," I say, laughing, and he puts one of his wonderful strong arms around my shoulders.

"Maybe you've never had a man, Miss McLeod," he says and it is just enough to make me wonder again.

Fortunately, when we get to that point, at least I think it's a point that things are getting interesting, something always seems to happen. The phone rings. Somebody walks in. We reach the end of the street and a pick-up takes away the moment. Or Phyllis walks in if it's at my office.

Roger Shutte has us wait about fifteen minutes, so I take advantage of the time to use the restroom and get myself a coffee. Jake apparently does the same. We sit quietly waiting our turn and when it finally comes, Roger Shutte says:

"I see things are a little better between you two than the last time." He opens the door to his office and the two of us go in.

"We've been working at overcoming our distance on this," I volunteer, knowing that as perceptive as Roger is he probably sees more than I do. Jake only smiles.

"I haven't had as much time as I need," Shutte continues, "but we have to take this to my conference room. The delay was a friend of yours, Jake. I've never been comfortable with him, and I put him in there." He nods toward the conference room. "I told him I need to meet with the two of you first since she's a lawyer and I am duty bound to her. She brought this to me. I made the decision to share. I don't want to regret that.

"He seems to think he has a right to her file. I don't. He's not going to get it from me. I don't push people around. How much of it has she let you see so far?"

"Not one friggin' page."

"In my view then," Shutte says. "It's hers and I think that's what a court would say."

"He's prepared to do that," Jake reveals, "more than prepared, he has already started the wheels turning in federal court."

He looks at me, apologetically and I quickly decide that was the conversation he disagreed with in the car on the way up.

The look I give him is not kind.

"Look I'm going to give you the quick version, then I'm gonna let you go and then send him on his way. I'll take the heat, I guess, till you get back to your office and prepare for the onslaught," he says primarily to Jake but the message is for me.

"No," I say. "Something is pressing here. We all know it. I think Sharon Donaldson is in danger. She thinks they need two weeks based on something McNelly said to her. She has had her hands on too much information. I am afraid of what they will do to her if she tries to fight them."

"You're the boss," Shutte says. "Let's go face the lion's den then."

The three of us go into Shutte's conference room and Jake's boss, Roy Flint is waiting. He's fairly famous in enforcement circles but no one outside that circle would consider him a power or a threat. He's a little guy. Wiry. A twerp, you would say, if maybe still in grade school. He does not exude friendliness.

"You know each other," Roger says.

"I haven't had the pleasure; but the man is a legend in his own time," I say and extend my hand purposely trying to flatter him. He looks up. Starts to extend his hand, then withdraws it. I pat his arm, my mother's thing, and he literally moves away from my touch.

So, I think. Message gotten. I sit.

"Let's get down to it," Roger says. "I've done an exhaustive study at your request, Shadow, and it doesn't look good to me. I am giving you this summary in the presence of these authorities because I have an additional arrangement with them that requires me to make them aware of anything that I consider to be a threat to national security. I consider this to meet that requirement and I called in the person I have traditionally met with and am comfortable that I have his confidence. But at this point I am being asked to do something that goes beyond what I am comfortable with and I don't have the final answer yet.

"Mr. Flint, I am not comfortable with pressure, given the way in which this information came to me, and had I believed the information …"

"He did not get it from me," Jake interjects. "It came to him from another source."

"Then he should deal with that other source," Roger Shutte says with finality. "I deal only with you."

"Then your arrangement with us is over," Flint says and it is not a question.

"So be it," Shutte says.

"I don't have a dog in that fight," I say. "But I do have people I want protected. Perhaps there is a way to reach a compromise we can all live with."

All three look at me as if they did not believe, first, that I had been there, or second, that I had the right or the ability to speak.

"If the gentleman shows me what he has, there may be no reason for me to worry about what I have. I could confirm that for him, if he likes. You can tell us what this means. And I can go back to my little legal practice in the sticks and go on with my life until I step on the wrong toes," I say.

The three of them talk.

The three of them talk as if I am not in the room.

The three of them reach a decision they will ask me what I have and they do so.

"Doesn't work that way," I say. "You show me yours; then I'll show you mine."

Again, the three of them confer.

Flint asks his first question: "You have it with you?"

"A copy," I say.

"And the original?"

"I don't have to disclose that to you."

"I have to see it all."

"Isn't that why your boy's there?" I ask, looking at Jake.

Flint hands me his folder. I have looked at this material in four formats now. First, with Fee Lo, although it had Babe's notes with it then. Second with Sharon Donaldson, and it had a major statement by Dr. David Dickerson that was not in the other set. I laid out the pages, just as Phyll and I had laid them out for copying. This is the same thing Sharon Donaldson put in my custody. I nod to Roger Shutte and he leaves us and returns after a while with my file. I let him hand it over to Flint to review. Not a word is different. But I have Dickerson's statement, the original of which is in my safe deposit box.

He leans back after returning my file to Roger.

I return his file to him.

"Give us the story," he says to Shutte, who turns on a screen and pulls up pretty much the same thing I had already looked at.

He puts on a graph that I have not seen and it summarizes chemical purchases at Rutter over a period of three months. "These increased daily," he says, "until they reached the top of the graph yesterday."

He goes to another graph.

"This one looks at the work being done, all in the East Field, based on these chemical purchases and based on his analysis of what each chemical does when combined with another."

He says not a word when he finishes showing us the last graph.

It is still largely Greek to me but for one thing. An over-abundance of saline is involved in the production.

"Saline can be a healing thing," Shutte says.

"The primary problem in the Middle East right now is the problem we will all have if we don't heed the call of the universe to clean up our act.

Water.

They have no natural clean water. They have enormous wealth and enormous development and can put snow slopes under glass in the desert for people to ski on; but they have no water. I am theorizing that the person who comes forward with water wins the prize.

"That's my guess about the area this involves. But something else is happening and I'm not ready to give you conjecture on that at this point. Something else is going on that makes this top secret for Rutter and given the conduct of sending everybody on furlough, ramping up action in R&D, increasing purchases I haven't seen since hearing about it from the Great War archives. It's not good."

He puts another graph on the screen.

"These are petroleum by products this company has used for a hundred years. But once it is produced here, on the very quiet side of Rutter right now, it disappears, I think into the East Side. And this is their secret."

"That's all folks," he says and just looks at us.

"Thank you, Roger," I say. "I need to get back to Houston. I trust you will return that where it goes and I will call you when I get back."

"You can't withhold information from us," Flint says.

"I haven't," I say. "I gave you something you didn't have and when you look closely at it, if you need a legal opinion, call me. I have nothing else for you," I say. "You've taken over protection of my client. I trust you will do it well. I will let you know, through your agent here, if anything else comes my way."

With that I retrieve my bag from the chair Jake put it on and start downstairs. I expect to be arrested. I don't care. I go to the sidewalk and call an Uber, which comes within minutes, and have it take me to Love Field, where a Southwest Airlines jet takes off for someplace almost every minute.

I am late in the line and sit somewhat toward the back in a threesome seat that has only the middle open. I put my bag up top and figure I can stew for an hour without saying a word to anyone and that's what I do despite my habit of using airline travel to practice voir dire skills by picking the person beside me apart until I know their entire life. That is not attractive at this point.

Once more in the life of Shadow McLeod, I am off men.

CHAPTER TWENTY-THREE
Looking for Dickerson

"Thanks for arranging the protection," I tell Roger that night. "I have a list of employees I'm faxing from a throw down phone." If you look it over, you may have the resources to know where these people came from. Using your friends there, you might be able to come up with a clearer picture of what's happening. I'm looking for two of them, the doctors who may have the ability to come up with the science. Look them over and tell me what you think."

I don't even bother to answer the other call when it comes.

By that time, Phyllis and I are back at Fee Lo's.

We check first to make sure we are the only ones there and we secure the lock that Phyl found yet another friend of Rand's to install for us. Rand sent him over so I'm assuming Rand is on for the ride.

In Fee Lo's apartment, we say nothing. We don't have much to say because we said what we needed to say in the car. In fact, we write notes to each other as we look into our assigned areas. Being something of a neatness freak when things get as messy as the way they left Fee Lo's loft, I decide to clean up just the mess that now has begun to draw vermin from the evidence of droppings. I run the sink full of water and start scraping the dishes one by one into a sack for trash and put in enough Dawn to start the process of soaking the residue off. Some of it is stuck as hard as egg yolk and seems pasted on permanently.

When I come to the large pot, I have worked myself into a corner. The sink is full. The pot is full, but I have to dig down and drain out enough water to take it out. While I am doing this, Phyllis silently pulls up the pot and drops it back in. I see her face turn ghostly white.

I plug the sink and help her with the pot, which is heavy but not that heavy. Beneath it we see what Fee Lo hid.

Saying not a word, we pour the water in the sink and while I replace the pot and the water that was in it, Phyl takes the contents and slides them into the neck of her shirt.

We have hit pay dirt and leave the dishes to soak.

We retrace our steps.

We mark out our footprints.

We relock the door.

We descend four flights of stairs.

We regain the car.

We take our first breath

"Holy Mother of God!" Phyllis says in exultation once the car door closes.

"Are we good? Or are we great?"

I just laugh and laugh.

. . .

Jake is waiting on the steps when we get back to our office.

. . .I motion him in and Phyl and I do as we routinely do.

Check the premises.

Secure the locks.

Lower the Shutters.

"It's better if you don't talk," I say and Phyllis gives us both a questioning look. She had asked about Dallas. I told her Shutte's opinion but none of the rest.

"You don't understand," he says.

"Oh but I do," I say. "I understand too well and you know it. Just don't let it get personal from now on."

He goes into my office and sits at my desk. I don't know why men do that but the desk, which my Mother bought for me—to give me courage, she said—does have a commanding presence. I turn on my Bose to Willie Nelson, then change it quickly to Degas, something less nature-tugging than good ole Willie.

I put on classical to cover my noticeable heavy breathing. I am angry but he already knows it.

Phyllis calls me to the back where she is going over my work on the cases she gave me to work on enroute to Dallas.

"I stayed here so you'd have to get close. I see I ruined it. You worked up every file."

I grimace.

"Give me what Fee Lo hid," I tell her.

"You gonna give it to him?"

"No I'm going over it with him. Like it or not, he's the only show in town. Where else are we going to go for help?"

She follows me back to my office and pulls in a chair. We leave Jake at the desk. I peel off each layer of Fee Lo's papers, read them and pass them on and we work like this, the three of us for more than an hour. Phyllis leaves to make copies of pages as we finish them and lays out three neat packages on her desk.

Jake leaves to use the restroom.

I see him observe the stacks.

I note he left his cell phone on the desk. That could either mean he is taping us and I point it out to Phyl or he wants us to trust him. Either way, the situation is tainted by my full understanding that his boss put him here to seduce me into cooperating.

I open a small individual pour bottle of Pinot Grigio. We are not going home, it's too late.

We work until we have discussed the papers and I am surprised that they get us no further than we were with the set Sharon Donaldson gave us.

I give Jake the list of employees.

"It would be helpful if you search these names. If it's anybody known to you, I would assume they might change their names. But you may have something that gives you country of origin. Sharon was certain they spoke no English in some cases and gave her a scrap of paper with their hours. All payments were made in cash. She didn't indicate an enormous amount of money. So it might be more than that and what they are paid in cash could be per diem. I know Rutter does that for overseas folks."

He studies the list at length.

"These two stand out," he said finally.

Well, of course, I think. They are PhDs. But I say nothing. Phyll looks at me over his shoulder because she is reading the list with him.

"Give him what we have," I say. "Maybe he can see if they can find out where they are."

She leaves to get the information. We have carefully taken our timeline down every time we leave the office. I rethink it and hang it so Jake can study it.

"You ever think of joining us?" he asks.

I just look at him as he continues reading. Phyl has a decidedly changed attitude that comes soon after the arrival of any male into our world. "I'm hungry, she says. Anybody for bacon and eggs?"

Jakes does a deep dive.

Neither of us ate all day. We had coffee and then coffee and then coffee.

Phyll leaves while he continues to read. We have a kitchen in the back because we often need it. Oddly, it's times just like this when we work late into the evening. Before long, we hear Phyll knocking around in the kitchen. She really can't cook, but she can reheat already cooked bacon, which is all we buy. And she can scramble or fry an egg. She makes a mean slice of toast in the toaster oven. It leads me to believe she does this often. By the time she calls us, she has set the table and the food is ready.

Jake puts his hand on my back when we walk back to the kitchen, and I move away.

"You have to let me explain," he says as we sit at the table.

"No need," I say flatly. "It just changes character. You've had that happen before. We need each other for this case. We're both adults. I'm cool with it."

"You don't know half as much as you think you do," he says and I waiver, because as always when a man criticizes me, I fall apart.

Phyll calls a truce.

"You two better eat the food I made or I will," she threatens and we laugh and join her at the table.

It is good. I don't have a lot of midnight breakfasts with guys. Despite the circumstances, I enjoy the handsome dose of testosterone. He even looks good when he eats. Sitting with his elbows on the table, holding toast as if he is questioning whether he wants the second piece Phyll made for him. And draining his cup.

"I have to go, Ladies," he says with what seems to be true regret. "I have to report to my boss before I sleep."

With that we say our goodbyes. Phyll gives him our schedule for the morning and we don't tell him we are going to look for Dr. David Dickerson in the afternoon.

CHAPTER TWENTY-FOUR
Visiting Dr. Dickerson's Friends

I plead two cases in the morning and we are through by noon.

When I get back to the office and park the Harley in its protected little alcove, I lock it up and go inside.

Phyll is ready for our journey. She spent the morning on the telephone and the computer. She has a list of places where Dickerson may be hiding. All are places he has worked before, including College of the Mainland, where we have a friend who teaches Biology and met Dickerson when they both examined moon rocks at NASA.

Emmeline Manske is still a good-looking woman. She was married to a colleague when I met her but for some years she did research at NASA. Seems Dickerson was there at the same time. We talk a bit and introduce ourselves again. She thinks she knows Phyll but can't imagine where until they discover Costa Rica, where both have been active in education for the native children.

She remembers me but totally dislikes the colleague she was married to then. I don't tell her that he was generally viewed to be a jerk by his co-workers. I don't say that; she did marry him after all and must have felt something for him at the time.

We finish cups of very bad coffee from a machine and finally get around to Dickerson and why we are looking for him.

"We were good friends," she says of Dickerson, "but I haven't seen him in years. Literally since the moon rocks. That's a long time."

She tells us he was a genuine guy, a decent scientist, not particularly ambitious in his science but honest.

I ask her what she means by that and she laughs.

"That's just like a lawyer," she says. "Yours is the only profession where honesty requires a definition. You mean how honest was he? Did he bend the rules? Was he a philanderer?

"I should have just asked," I said, because I had obviously lost the rapport that grew out of her benevolent friendship with Phyll. "Were you casual or more than that," I ask, not being nosy but wanting to ask in as kind a way as possible because, I've heard about the things men seem inclined to give up in bed and after sex.

"Probably more than casual, never serious," she says. "Frankly, we were scientists with different goals and attitudes about life.

"I've always wanted to teach," she explains. "Dickerson's an inventor; a nice guy though," she adds. "He has a sense of mission with his work. It can make you money, but first it has to benefit mankind. Not all of them are like that and you know it. This other guy you ask me about, I don't know him; but the name is familiar. I will look him up. See if there's anything out there."

I hand her a card and she writes Phyllis' name and number on it as well.

The point is well taken.

We start to leave.

"I did see him again," she says stopping us. "I wonder why I forgot about that, but I must have purposely put it away. It's a big thing too. He picked me up one Friday afternoon, having asked me to spend the weekend with him. We drove a God-awful number of miles, far West of San Antonio; but not quite to El Paso territory," She stops as if to remember.

"Middle of nowhere actually. He'd bought land for a ranch and wanted a good-spirited woman to help him look it over. I guess I should have been flattered. We camped. He had all the goods. I was more patient than enthralled and we left early on that Sunday to come back." She then looked at me and grinned.

"Funny thing. He couldn't wait to fuck under the moonlight, and we did, hard ground and all. He obviously had fantasized two people in a single sleeping bag. Actually, it was fun! Then, no action the rest of the time. Can't imagine I would forget that, but I did, until this moment. I don't even know if he bought that land although I was a good girl and told him the expected—that I did not think he could go wrong if he did. It already had a pumping well on it!"

We said our goodbyes with promises to call with any new memories or information.

Phyll didn't say a word about my fumbling method with people;

but she did pick up the list and told me who was next closest on it.

This time we were at NASA, which seems like a ghost of its former vital self. We go through the gate, pass the Challenger Park, drive around the main building and end up on the back side and a string of doors that appear to be rows of offices opening to the outside.

CHAPTER TWENTY-FIVE
The NASA Women

Our next stop is to see Tilly Park and Samantha Hook, both NASA scientists. Both are long-time bureaucrats and both remember Dr. David Dickerson very well.

"I haven't thought of him in quite a while," Samantha Hook says. She seems to be surrounded by folder after folder, each full of papers. Petite. Brown hair turning gray in streaks, she is soft spoken and seems shy. She looks up as we walk in after knocking. She seems glad to see us.

"I would love to know what you do that causes those mountains of papers by you," I say.

She laughs, good-naturedly and slides one stack aside to make more room.

"That's just me, I need to be surrounded by my work before I can think."

"And what kind of thinking do you do," I ask, although I see Phyl getting anxious.

"Oh, I am a systems analyst, which means if there were a related system, say in the space shuttle, they might bring to me a particular question about performance or ideas to change it and I would have to pass on its effect on everything in the system before it could move on."

"And is that what Dr. Dickerson did?" I ask.

"Oh, no," she says. "David actually designed the systems that I analyzed and we saw each other often because virtually everything he did, I had to look at."

"Sounds complicated."

"Well it is and it isn't. You might say he designed the living apparatus for the, what we were working on then, Challenger. How they stored their meals. How they got rid of their meals both from packages and from their bodies. How we kept their water pure despite its being re-circulated."

"I hope that doesn't mean what I think it means."

"Oh, it does, in part."

"That was his big thing, you know. Water. Keeping it pure."

I felt the tug of something Shutte had said and know it will come back.

"Can you show me what he drew for Challenger?"

"I'm not sure. I'm sure I could but they may not let me. Since those O-rings froze and did the damage they did, everybody is real sensitive about design and Challenger.'

"It might be important to helping us find him, I think. What kind of person was Dickerson?"

"Oh, the very best," she says. "If I thought for a minute you weren't on his side, I would not have opened the door. He stood up for me on a matter that I will always be grateful for."

"Can you share?"

"Not easily. Let me look up the water design for you on Challenger. I'll send it to this address she gave me if it's not closed off to you. If it is, I'll call you. You can always come back and I can show you how to get it under open records."

We thank her and move on down the drive to Tilly Park's office.

Tilly Park looks like she can be a piece of work. She has dreads about two feet long wrapped around her head. They are bright orange/red and almost glow. Her skin in as smooth looking as peeled Avocado and has about the shade of yellow found in the seed. She has glasses on her nose and is wearing a shocking pink stretch t-shirt under her white jacket that announces her as a PhD. Her nails are at least a half-inch over the ends of her fingers, and she stops typing and stands to greet us, stretching her fingers as if she has been at it for a while. She is resourceful looking and quite attractive.

I let Phyll take the lead; they seem like a matched set.

"We are here about David Dickerson. I called," she says.

"Yes, you did girlfriend and because he's one of my all-time favorite Dudes, I will talk to you. Otherwise I'd tell you to move on because what they did to that Dude here was wrong and it still gets into my craw! Sit, ya'all, I got to finish this email and then I can talk.

"You can read this while you wait," she says handing Phyll the file. "I pulled some stuff for you. Sam called me to let me know what you want. I have it 'cause I was an intern for him and happened to be on that project. She says if this is not what you need, then come back to see her. Dr. Dickerson took up for both of us and he took the blame by filing the complaint to keep them off our backs. Not them," she concedes, "an asshole we had to work with who thought women lived for the chance to give him a blow-job. Prick!"

She giggles. "We were damn near ready to cut off his dick!"

Without further information, she returns to her computer and starts typing again.

Phyll passes the file to me with a knowing glance I can't read; and I open it so that we can both look at it at the same time. I'm getting accustomed to Dickerson's scribbles and his symbols and his references to chemicals by symbols. Not that I can read them any better; but I could certify these are his because of their close similarity to the things we have. I turn the papers over to stop on one page and show it to Phyll. I see that her reaction is similar to mine. We have seen at least a portion of this page before. I watch Tilly and see her reach the end, reread her email and then hit send. She turns to us.

"This page," I say, showing her the one I am looking at, "Can you tell me what this is?"

She takes it and looks at it and shifts back two or three pages and then looks up.

"Well this doesn't specifically come from Challenger," she explains. "This was something Dr. Dickerson was working on. I helped on it, but it didn't go anywhere because its time had just not come. They are actually using these in some places right now; and I saw an article on one in Africa just the other day and wondered if Dr. David got the patent rights, because I lost track of him altogether. He should have them for sure. This was his design." She looks a few other pages ahead and then goes back to the one we marked.

"I can't remember exactly why this is here, to tell you the truth. I know we worked on one; but nobody was to be on the surface of anything long enough to need this. We put one together, Dr. Dave and I. This one might not have worked, because I don't see where he designed the container for it," she says, flipping through the other pages, I assume, to find a container design. "There's not one."

Then she adds: "But it's a portable water system. You can actually fold up this baby and carry it under your arm when you have to. No question about it working just as he said. They used one just this week in Africa. Village was too remote. Water system collapsed. This system can be put in place immediately with gas driven generators and for almost no money whatsoever, it gives them pure water. At least it serves the immediate need. Wow, I forgot all about this after the o-rings froze. The shit literally hit the fan around here. Astronauts petitioned like crazy for cardinal safety rules that had to be enforced. Sally Ride, that darling, resigned, although they begged her not to, but I thought it was in protest because she lost so many of her friends."

"Tell me about Dr. Dave. Were you close or casual?"

She looked at me as if she was about to get angry. "Would we have gone to him for help with a blow-job demanding jerk, if he was the type to bonk an intern? Don't think so, Darlin'. He was more than close to both of us, but we never fucked, if that's what you're asking."

"I'm very sorry," I say, "I never meant that as an insult. I am just trying to find somebody that got under his skin who could help me figure out what he might be doing. This is confidential, but he gave very important papers to a little woman he worked with and then he disappeared. There may be a woman with him. I'm just at a dead-end street."

"Darlin' you don't have to apologize. It just shook me 'cause I had a major crush on Dr. Dave. I would have done it with him. Maybe that's what makes me angry. That I didn't."

"Ok," she adds, "where can he be?"

She studies the wall over my head.

"You might want to check out that house he has at Tiki. Sam and I went there to talk to him. Other than that, I have no idea."

We hug rather than shake hands. She makes us a copy of everything she says is in that file that relates to the page we want and we leave.

"Shit," I tell Phyll as soon as we got in the car.

"Where to from here?" she says.

CHAPTER TWENTY-SIX
Two More Women

We had two other stops but it was getting past office hours. We called the first one and she said for us to meet her at her home in an hour. The other one said come now and I'll wait for you.

"You notice a pattern, here?" I ask Phyll. "Dr. Dickerson's close friends are all women."

"Well, he seems like a nice man."

"Right."

"You think Babe just might have taken off with him?" Phyll asks.

"Well, it's certainly something I think she would do," I say.

"Might be safer than staying around."

"Do you think Fee Lo is with them?" Phyll asks.

I shake my head.

"Somehow, I think three would be a crowd and that he is doing something else or can't."

We make our other two visits. Neither has any idea where Dickerson could be. One had not talked to him in ten years. Neither knew where he lived in the first place but remembered a get together at his house at Tiki Island.

Both had the most recent contact and worked with him on engineering projects at Rutter. Sheila Jonas said he was the number one design engineer when she was at Rutter and that he was on first name basis with all the upper echelon, which included the oldest of the original owners remaining on site. Jeremiah Rutter was a great-great-grandson of the founder and bore the same name. He was a prissy little man, who walked with a silver-topped-cane although he didn't need it, combed his hair back straight from his face and wore it in a modified pompadour. He had a man bun before they were fashionable.

"That man did nothing day after day but walk the halls, tossing his cane against everybody's door, saying good morning and going on. He not only did not do any work, he did not know how to do any work related to the company.

"He was a money man and his sole concern was the price of the stock and how much money Rutter Industries put away that year.

"If you couldn't talk to him about that," Sheila adds. "He didn't need to talk to you. I do remember he introduced Dr. Dickerson personally around the plant when he came to Rutter, saying Rutter would right a wrong to a Great American, who had gotten us to the moon and back, although Dr. Dickerson repeatedly emphasized that he was not designer of the moon program. His was Challenger."

"How well were you and Dr. Dickerson acquainted," I ask, trying to be careful.

"Oh, we were close," Sheila explains. "Dr. Dickerson was head of my section. I would still be there but they transferred him out and I just didn't like the climate after that."

"Were you close enough to know anybody he might have sought out in the event something became dangerous?" I ask.

"I can't imagine that circumstance," Sheila says. "Dr. Dickerson was just not the type to dabble in intrigue."

"There was a man," she adds. "His name was Goose—that wasn't his name of course, but that's what Dr. Dickerson called him. Goose lived on Dr. Dickerson's ranch way out in West Texas and did upkeep. He was a local. Talked like a local. I never saw him. I can picture him in my mind from talking to him on the phone when Dr. Dickerson was headed that way. I'd tell Goose to open up and get it ready. And he always, without fail, said, Oh it's already ready! Stays that way. From what I heard, his view of ready and Dr. Dickerson's view were two different things."

"Do you remember where it is," I asked. "Or the number you called."

She frowns and looks up to her left as if it will float by.

"Oh, no," she says. "I've found lately I have no memory at all."

"Did you ever go there?"

"No, that was not something we did. I only remember Goose because he was such a character it came through on the phone. And I usually had to make the call once Dr. Dave decided to go to the ranch."

"If you looked at a map of the area," Phyll interjects. "Would it possibly remind you?"

"I don't mind trying," she says and takes Phyll's phone and scrolls through an area West of San Antonio off Interstate ten and East of El Paso. She does this for a while and then hands it back. "Nothing comes up."

Our last person is nearby. Phil explains she also worked at Rutter when Dr. Dickerson was there and no longer does, just like Sheila.

"You did a great job of tracking these people," I say sincerely. "I don't know how you do it."

"A nose for nosey," she says. "This one is Doris Stuart. She lives in Webster, just East of NASA. We drive to the subdivision, which is a very nice community with oversized oaks dripping with heavy branches loaded with moss. A few people are out walking dogs, I guess after supper, and we pull up to Stuart's house and Phyll pulls into the yard and parks behind a small BMW coupe.

We get out.

Doris Stuart meets us at the door.

"It's a nice night for sitting out back," she says. And it was. She has chairs on a patio and a brick walkway that leads to this nice sitting area by a strip of water leading to the Bay. She has red and white wine in containers and has glasses, cheese and crackers ready. Something hangs from a tree to deal with mosquitos.

"This is very nice, thank you," I say and introduce myself and Phyllis, who has already explained what we are doing; and I notice that Doris Stuart has a file lying on a table by her chair.

"I took the chance and made you some copies of things that I have from my time with David," she says.

"This was at Rutter?"

"Yes, and we worked together on about five major projects in that many years. He was a hard worker, and I kept these reminders of what we did together because I was proud; but also because I thought I might need them in looking for a new job if Rutter got to be more than what it was getting to be. I knew I would have to leave if it did. When the older guys passed on and this last grandson came into power, the mission at Rutter seemed to change and I personally thought it was not his doing but that he was so subject to being manipulated that it was easy for people, who had wanted for a long time to modernize

Rutter, to convince him that was what he wanted to do."

She sips her wine and offers us a small tray with cheese and crackers.

"Bless his heart," she adds. "He just couldn't help it. David saw it and I saw it and we talked about it many times. It was particularly disturbing to David because of what happened to him at NASA and Challenger. He had that dumped on him when it was not a design situation at all—we thought it was pure politics and management error!" She takes another sip and puts the glass back on the table.

"I can't give you anything else," she says. "I know you want to know where he might be. If I knew, I probably would not tell you if it opens him up to more danger. I loved David. I still love David. I would not help you put him in danger for anything."

I felt whipped with a kid glove.

"Wow!" I say. "We clearly haven't thought that out. I certainly don't want to bring danger to him. I want my friend and I want his friend back. I am so afraid they have met danger and that Dr. Dickerson would know what to do. We can leave," I say. "I'm sorry we put you through this."

"There was a nice part of it," she says. "It let me go into these papers and see what we did together. We were a great business team. We made that company a lot of money. And we did it the right way, if you know what I mean by that. Our work was good and Rutter was good then. Now, I hate to think about it."

"Do you have any explanations for what is happening to Rutter?"

"Just a major change in philosophy," she says. "Most of us in an earlier time liked getting paid nice salaries but it was not our quest to just make money. We thought we were helping mankind. I don't know where that is coming from now but the bottom line is all they care about.

"Can you at least tell us where the ranch is?" I ask.

"Ranch?" she asks. "I don't know about a ranch."

I cannot tell whether she is being truthful or lying through her teeth; but I can tell the interview is over. I thank her for the hospitality and the file without opening it and Phyll and I leave.

In the car, I deflate.

"I never thought about that," I tell Phyll. "If we find these two people, we've done something Rutter couldn't do. Do you think they followed us today?"

"We didn't tell anybody where we were going," she says. "Not even Jake or Rand. How could they know we were up to something?"

"Did you call them from the office?"

"Half of them I called from home. Nobody could know me from Adam."

"Which three?" I ask.

"I have to look at it," Phyll says. "I'll call tomorrow on a throw down and see if anybody's bothered them."

"I think we should and I think we should tell Jake to put somebody on them if he can."

CHAPTER TWENTY-SEVEN
Jake Makes his Move

Once more, Jake is waiting on the steps of the office when we get there.

"I've got to go home or I won't make it tomorrow," Phyll says, dropping me off at the office. I get out with our files and start up the steps; but Jake gets up to take them.

He walks her to her car and tells Phyll, goodnight. I think I see her wink, but that's no good.

She yells: "You're not due in court until 10. The files are on your desk."

"Good night, Honey," I say. "Thank you for everything. You're the greatest!"

She drives off and I can tell she wants to get away before she changes her mind.

And she does.

And Jake stands by me until I open the door, dutifully holding the files and our papers.

He checks things out just as Phyll and I would do and then he goes by them, one by one and closes all the shutters.

I divide up the files and go to the restroom and then the kitchen to make us a coffee.

When I come back, he surprisingly, is respecting my space, but he has the feet on the corner of the desk, without his boots, and he has Willie Nelson on the Bose.

I can feel the heartache coming on and hand him the coffee.

"If we're gonna work, I need to turn that off," I say and I do so.

I go over the files on the women with him, one by one.

"I don't want to call Roger until morning but I think we got two important clues with what we did today."

He waits silently.

"First, Dr. Dickerson is a good guy. The people Phyll found who worked with him closely are all women. Two minorities. One school-teacher. One retired engineer and one working engineer. All think he hung the moon. He did something special and great for each one of them. They know he had a house at Tiki. You've gone through it, I'm sure. Maybe if Phyll and I went through it with you, we could find what you missed.

"My two good leads for Roger are that Dickerson designed a portable water system. The reason I think it might be related is the drawing you see here and what we have already seen. One of his co-workers explained to me ...".

"Shadow, this could be it," Jake interrupts and moves forward in his seat at my desk. "You have this also?"

"I do, I can't get to it tonight because Phyll hid it. We don't talk on the phone anymore. We are afraid we are putting people in danger."

He leans back. Smiles.

"You are the smartest woman I've ever known."

"And beautiful." He adds.

"Don't," I say. "You played me for that asshole you work for. He thinks you get to me because I'm working with you, doing my dead level best to help you accomplish exactly what you need. But the chance we could have what I thought we could have is none. I have little left in this case except my pride and you have stepped on it!"

I throw the papers at him and leave the room.

"Look at that on your own. I will stay until you finish."

I go into the kitchen and make a peanut butter and jelly sandwich, my comfort food in times of stress. And I pour myself a big glass of very cold Skim Milk.

I feel his presence before he gets there and know that he is on the way. I stiffen involuntarily but he comes in any way and puts his hands on my shoulders. But he does not move into my space.

"My favorite thing in all the world is a peanut butter and grape jelly sandwich. My Mother used to make them for me because she knew whatever was wrong with my world, it would suddenly be okay."

"You can have this one."

"But she would eat one with me," he says. "I can't eat it alone."

I start laughing and smear the peanut butter on one slice and add jelly to the other. I put the sides together and smush them the way I like. I grab a paper towel and turn to put the sandwiches on them; but he takes them from me, then licks his fingers. I can't help it! I smile at him as he pulls out my seat.

"Allow me," he says to me, taking his first bite before he takes the chair on the other side of the table. He holds the sandwich away from his face. "Wow, I am in love with anybody who can make a sandwich this good." He takes another bite, obviously loving it. He never says another word until he finishes the sandwich. He also drinks a glass of milk.

"My compliments to the chef," he says and stands up and bows to me. "Mademoiselle, May I have your hand in marriage?"

"You are truly hopeless," I say.

"No," he says. "I am now convinced that after forty years of having no one who made a peanut butter and jelly sandwich like that but my Mother, the Gods smiled on me and now tell me that there is another, who can do the same. Alexandra Shadow McLeod, you may not believe it; but you will someday be my wife."

With that he sits back down.

"Now eat your sandwich," he said, persuasively, as you might talk to a child. I dutifully comply; I am hungry after all. When we finish, he gets up and wipes off the table, closes up the peanut butter and jelly and puts it in the cabinet I have left open.

"We don't want anything to happen to this," he says. "I did the dishes," he says. "My Dad always said that to my Mother and then he waited by the sink for her to reward him. He stands by the sink. Waiting. The same smile is on his face.

My body stands up and says, "Yes, Sir. Here I am." That's not me talking, you understand; that is my body.

I stand up and cross the room like a woman in a trance and lift my face for him to kiss me. Whatever I intended, I am not left wanting. Jake, the lawman, has not forgotten how to kiss.

He kisses.

Then he kisses me again.

Then he kisses me again until I pull away.

"Oh, Wow," I say. "Did you have to do that so well?"

"Oh, yes, I put my best effort in it, and I am prepared to do it again." He moves in and like a total slut I am all over him.

I was thinking that I wished I could tell you that one thing led to another; but Jake's phone rang incessantly until he answered it and it was Flint the Bastard making demands.

"Your timing is for shit," he says and turns off the phone. But the magic is gone.

"I have to go home tonight," I say. "I'm tired; I need to stretch out on my own bed."

"If I promise to sleep on the couch, will you let me go with you?"

"That ain't gonna happen," I say.

"Which part? I can't go with you or you won't let me sleep on the couch if I get you there?"

I shake my head. "I'm a big girl, Jake. I'll be okay."

"It's an Order," he says. "We've already sent Rand to Phyllis, which he willingly did; and she is in for the night. Old Flint says I have to stay with you until I bring you to him tomorrow. He's convinced you found what we need."

"And how would he know?" I ask; but I don't really want to hear that answer.

As a matter of fact, one thing did lead to another. The morning after I knew life had changed; and I never wanted to get out of bed again.

CHAPTER TWENTY-EIGHT
Work Goes On

Phyll must have gotten a hint about what had happened because she called at 9:30 and said, "Do I need to go to Court for you?" I actually consider it; but finish off the toast he made while I showered and threw on my clothes.

"I'll get you there on time," he says as we lower the shutters on my little beach house, which would never be the same again, and I grab my files for work. I am acutely aware of his presence on the back row of every court I have to go to until we finish and he heads toward my office. Since he never leaves my side between Courts, it becomes pretty obvious to everyone that I have an escort.

Stevens asks: "Are you about to be arrested?"

"Something like that," I say and smile. But I notice that he does not smile when he observes my escort waiting on the back row.

We go over what we have with Flint and I tell him I want to call Roger Shutte while he is there.

"No," he says. "You complicate things between us."

"It's too late for that," I say. "You don't play fair anyway and I don't like that." And Phyll hands me a phone already connected to Roger Shutte.

"Did you get your copy of what we got?" I asked. I knew that the first thing Phyll did was fax it to him. I am as anxious to see what he says as I was about getting the document in the first place. I go over with him as much as I can remember about the plans and what the lady said she had read about the one in Africa in the village that had a water failure.

"It's a good job, Shadow," he says on the speakerphone. "This might tie it all together. For one thing, I also thought they were missing a container for this machine. She tags that correctly, unless that is part of the plan. They have a partner using a different type of machine cover. I will check out the Africa machine and see who did it."

"We already have," Flint says, butting in.

"Thank you, Roger," I said. And then I hand the phone to Flint.

He is not happy; but he behaves, and I leave the room so they can talk.

"Did you call Sharon last night?"

"I did," she says. "No answer again. Rand and I are driving over there this afternoon for a professional call on Mother."

She winks and I go to the kitchen for more coffee.

CHAPTER TWENTY-NINE
Still Looking for Dickerson

While Jake is occupied with his boss, I call my friend Emmeline and ask her to put on her thinking cap.

"What's up?" she asks.

"I need to find that ranch," I say. "Try to remember. You remember the drive but try to remember the landmarks. You know you went I 10?"

"Yes," she says. "No doubt about that?"

"And you know you passed San Antonio?"

"Passed San Antonio, Yes," she says.

"And you know you never got to El Paso?"

"Yes, never got even near El Paso."

"Yes, never near El Paso."

"Okay, that leaves us about 400 miles to figure out. Was there a store near where you camped?"

"No, he had everything with him. I was surplus, he could have done it all by himself except the fucking. He was pretty much by himself anyway after the starlight fuck, which I think he was fixated on."

"How far off I 10 was it?"

"Not," she says. "Not at all. It was there, pretty close, less than a mile and it had a dirt road packed into two stripes leading to it."

"Can you see it? By memory?"

"Yes, I can see it and I remember that he stopped to open a gate that crossed that same path; but he still wasn't on the place we camped. We drove into some scrub and it might even have been huisache."

"That is… huisache …?"

"A small tree that grows in West Texas but more to the South than where we were. I was surprised. It's related to the acacia plant."

What else did you see that surprised you?

"Deer. Deer so tame they walked right up to the campsite with us in it. Stood. Picked things off our stuff and then went on their way. They didn't seem to know people, but somebody put up the fence. So they must have."

"What else," I ask?

"I don't know how they lived," she said. "There was no water for miles. No creeks. Whatever was alive had to survive on rainwater because none flowed anywhere."

"So real dry and real West Texas. Dust?"

"Lots of it."

"Back to I 10, what was the last thing you remember seeing before he turned off?"

"Oh, I actually slept for a while. Maybe an hour. Which I can do in a car because I put my feet up on the dash and lean my chair back and enjoy the hum of the engine."

"So we cover your napping with at least 60 miles West of San Antonio during the hour you slept. Then what?"

"We had to stop so I could pee and get a Diet Coke?"

"And that was about how far?"

"Another thirty minutes, probably, because he wanted to stop one time and get gas and then he said we would be close."

"So with another 30 minutes added to the 60 that you slept we are now 90 miles West of San Antonio. I look at the map. Does Leakey ring a bell?"

"We passed the sign and there was a sprinkling of lights nearby and I said my bladder was going to be getting pretty Leakey, itself, if he didn't stop."

"Good job, Emmeline. We now know for certain it is at least West of Leakey. What next?"

"He said, Leakey's not the stop I want. Can you hold it? I said yes and I asked him where he planned to stop."

"Did you pass Fort Bliss?"

"I'm not sure?"

"Did you see notices of Donald Judd's sculpture?

"Let me think on that one. I would remember that; I kept a Journal for a long time while we were working on moon rocks. I'll check it out. I will call you, because I know it's important to you."

"Thanks, Honey," I say and hang up the phone.

Jake is standing over my shoulder. Funny how I can sense him before he gets to me.

"Any luck?" he asks.

"How broad was the warrant you had to go through Dickerson's house?"

He doesn't answer.

"I see," I say. "Can you get one?"

"Maybe, on what basis?"

"Something just tells me we need to check out the possibility that he got away and went to his ranch. They could all three be there until this blows over. I know we don't have much time. I think whoever is behind this at Rutter is on the verge of doing what they are planning to do. What did Flint say about the African water situation?"

"We are on top of it. Can't say anything more yet."

"You people treat life like a one-way street," I say but when I look up Jake just smiles.

CHAPTER THIRTY
Dickerson is Still a Mystery

I make a run to the *Enterprise* morgue again. Susan Miller takes the names I give her and brings me a handful of files. I open them and start reading. I look up the two former Rutter engineers and neither seems to have any hidden surprises out there. I look back through the NASA thing with Dickerson and if the *Enterprise* is to be believed, Dickerson is a great American hero and welcomed to the local Rutter Industries with open arms. Despite the number of articles, and Dickerson has a double file, not one mentions the Dickerson Ranch.

I give up and take the files back to Susan Miller, who notes they are returned in Alphabetical order, and thanks me. We say goodbye.

I have nowhere else to go and ask Jake if we can get a warrant on Dickerson's house.

"You really think it's that important?" he asks.

"At least let me satisfy that curiosity, so I can mentally go on to something else," I say.

He comes back with a Warrant signed by my favorite Judge Raleigh, the newest federal judge in our area.

Tiki island is a small subdivision on an island North of the Bay with better than middle class houses. Dickerson has a nice one. It's on a canal and he has a boat that is elevated at the dock. It swings over the canal.

Jake picks the lock and opens the door, I imagine he is using the same access he used before when he probably did not have a warrant.

I know what I'm looking for and I'm really not trying to invade the man's privacy, although I don't feel right going into his house. It is an emergency, I think, and it is because I think he's in danger, which is probably what Jake used as a reason to get Judge Raleigh to grant it. Fear of someone's physical condition is a valid reason for entry. I don't even look at the warrant as long as he tells me he has it.

Phyll, of course, is right here with me. It would not be acceptable to her for me to carry out a breaking and entering without sharing with her. I take one side of the house and give her the other. Before we have searched five minutes, she calls me into Dickerson's bedroom, which turns out to be on her side. Pretty fair division since I got his home office.

He has a small picture in a frame of what looks like land in the Texas dessert. It is an aerial from a small aircraft and shows fenced land, with a very small cabin on it. We look at the date in the corner and it is recent enough for Emmeline to have been on that exploration trip with him and time enough for him to buy it and build that cabin. I take it out of the frame to see if anything is written on the back. He—or someone—has scribbled: Goose Heaven

I take pictures of the front and back, restore picture to frame and Phyll rehangs it on the narrow wall by his shower. Intimate location, I think, and decide that's a clue.

In the office, I find no file folders with deeds or anything of the sort, whether of the Tiki Island House or the ranch and decide that he must have a safe somewhere and we discover that by and by in the closet of his bedroom, somewhat disguised on the back wall behind two racks of clothes. We do not try to open it.

Something in his life is private to Dr. Dickerson.

Something in his life, he chooses to hide.

And it has something to do with that ranch, but I have no idea what.

We continue to look. I need an address or some landmark that tells me where that cut off is. But it is not forthcoming. All we have is the photograph and I make sure the copy in my camera is good and ask Phyll to take another from her phone, which she does.

Jake agrees to take it and send it to his office for enlargement. So we take another one on his phone and he emails it to Flint and Roger Shutte.

I know Flint won't tell us, but he may have some way of identifying who owns all the land in West Texas if he needs to.

Phyll goes back to the office and Jake drops me off at the Courthouse with my files. When will you be ready to be picked up?" he asks.

"I can get a ride if you need for me to."

"No, I'm under orders. I have to watch you. I just believe you are safe enough at the Courthouse since I've now seen how all these cops around here give you the once-over whenever you pass. I can go to my office and pick up the enlargement and then come back by to get you. You have one court case, right?"

"Right," I say. "Okay, but let me know if you need for me to get a ride."

We go our separate ways.

I do another plea with Edward Stevens and he asks me where my bodyguard is and I smile and shake my head and put the file between us.

"I need Deferred on this case, really bad," I tell Stevens. "You get his plea of guilty if it goes South on him and he gets a second chance. It's a bad case, I concede, but I did have him do thirty AAs before I even asked. He has a sponsor and the sponsor tells me they are talking every time the kid has even an inkling of an idea that he needs a drink or drugs. We have the device on his car and his parents won't let him drive anything else. They are watching him like a hawk."

"This is Texas, Miss McLeod, you know I can't do deferred on DWI. I will do probation."

"He is so young. You can do Deferred if you amend the indictment."

"And have Mrs. Henny on my back. No thank you."

"Then reset it, please," I ask. The problem is that he is right and I know it.

I level with him: "These people go to Phyllis's church and she wants this one badly. She knows she can save him."

"Let me talk to Mrs. Henny," Stevens says, returning the papers to his file.

"Are you available for dinner? I have something I'd like to run by you." I would ask why Edward Stevens suddenly gets the nerve to ask me out, but he looks so damn serious, I decide it's probably business, although dinner seems more formal and less business than lunch.

Nature, of course, is a woman.

Does she rule that the presence of having one man available sets off the male pheromones and makes them all hover to see if their territory is being invaded? He seems frustrated and I stand there until he settles down.

"Guess not," he says.

"No, not that; I was just trying to think about what I have tonight. Phyllis usually lets me know when I leave what I have to come back to. We have both been so busy, we don't know if we are coming or going. "Yes, I can do dinner if you agree it will be an early evening. Can you pick me up at my office?"

And it goes unsaid he will not be taking me home.

Why do I do this to myself, I ask as I go down the front steps and out to Jake's car.

Well, it's done, I decide and I can deal with the consequences later.

We go back to the office but Jake hands me the envelope that holds a very enlarged copy of the aerial picture in Dickerson's bathroom.

"The house looks a little more able to support human life," I say as I look at his copy closely. "I didn't see that reflection in my copy or on the original for that matter. Can you see what it is? Looks almost like a double exposure."

"I can't but the technician did. It's a reflection; it shows Dickerson, himself."

I look at it. "Dickerson is flying the plane."

"Do you recognize the reflection to the side of him. Is it a woman sitting beside him."

"Can you print that better?"

"Look at the next one," he says. "See if you recognize that face?"

I take out the additional copy and look over at him.

I have no doubt whatsoever. The woman whose image is reflected sitting beside Dickerson in the small plane is Babe. My mind is doing double duty. This shows that Babe was alive and well and in the company of Dickerson three months ago, an event he felt so charmed by, he had her take the aerial of the ranch he was showing her and he hung it for himself only. It's like one of those ancient monarchs, having a room in which to enjoy his nude paintings of his women, although they settled for nothing less than Goddesses.

"It's Babe," I say.

And I do not tell him; but I have seen a painting that shows a scene so similar it could be the same place; but this one is a nice oil in Roger Schutte's office.

CHAPTER THIRTY-ONE
Double Date

I was so excited about having Phyll confirm my sighting of Babe and looking up the date printed on the small photograph to see what we were doing on that date to try to get some memory that would tell us where Fee Lo was when she is flying off with Dr. Dickerson, that I forgot that Edward Stevens was picking me up for dinner.

Phyll says something about raining and pouring and makes a beeline with him for the kitchen when he arrives.

I stand there between them and quickly decide it is business as usual. I grimace and smile. I decide the less I say by way of explanation the better. They can figure it out. After introductions, I ask Stevens: "Would you like a glass of wine or a beer before we go? I need to do a couple of things before I can leave."

Phyll and I have a routine before we close up for the night. I return files to her desk so that she'll know what happened; I pick up what she has for me, which is work for the next day. Sometimes she has a note and sometimes not, but she will hang around until I get through the stack. Then she usually leaves a bit ahead of me because she usually has an interest of her own to check out, which is my double-speak for date since I usually have none.

Stevens follows Phyll to the kitchen; Jake is behind me, and he closes the door as we go into my office.

"This is uncomfortable," he says. "I actually feel a little jealous."

"Don't," I say.

"Well," he says and I can tell something is on his mind that is not jealousy.

"What's wrong?"

"Other than the fact you're about to go out with another man?"

"You know life goes on, right?"

"This is a little hard," he says, pulling a paper from his shirt. It is folded and he unfolds it. I can tell it's a legal document but can't read it from the distance between us.

"It's an Order, placing you under my protection."

"What?"

"Your favorite Judge Raleigh signed it. You're under my protection. And your office. I have to keep you safe."

"You're kidding me?"

"No. Phyllis too. I was trying to find a way to tell you that wouldn't set you off."

"I give up. This goes from bad to worse. First I find out you're tracking us, with an Order, and now this. Does this have anything to do with last night?"

"Part of it."

"Do I dare ask?"

"Not the part that matters."

"Well that's something. If I find out you're lying, you will need to watch your back ten ways from Sunday." I nod smugly: "I have friends in low places."

"This is Flint. Not me. You set him off by standing up to him and he's on you like a tick on a hound primarily because you worked him over. But there is also something going on here that's bigger than us. And Rutter. It could be Rutter's in real trouble. It could be your friend and his woman are in worse trouble than that. A woman who has been ours for some time, quite innocently at first, but now with knowledge of what it's about has gone missing. Flint says you and your kickass sidekick, as she calls herself, may be next in line."

"I'll tell him …"

"Flint?"

"No. Edward Stevens."

"You have a thing with him?"

"I didn't. He just asked today and said he needed to talk with me about something. He seemed troubled. I said yes to dinner."

"How's he gonna feel when I go along?"

"Why don't we just ask him?" I sigh in exasperation.

And that's what I did. Without any explanation of the pending crisis, I tell Edward Stevens, I can give him a rain check; but that if we go to dinner, my bodyguard has to go with me. And Phyllis.

Edward Stevens looks Jake over. "I'm not that easy to get rid of," he says, looking in Jake's direction.

CHAPTER THIRTY-TWO
Traffic Jam

The next morning I get dropped off at the Courthouse again. Flint has ordered Jake to go behind us and visit each of the women we met the day before. Flint is certain, the FBI will pick up information we did not get.

Phyll has stacked me up with work and I don't have time to think about Fee Lo and Babe or Jake and the fact that I wonder if the scent of sex so permeates me that people will be able to look at me and sense the totally satiated way that I feel. And that has been a long time coming. I know coaches tell players to keep the zipper closed until after the game because they want no loss of mojo before the big game. And now I understand why.

Fortunately, I exhaust three of my cases before I run into Stevens in Pruser's Court. Lilly Pruser is new to the felony bench, having just won a hotly contested special election to fill the seat Judd Baker retired from, which would be a promotion at the same time. I have seen her in county court, with misdemeanors but have not yet had a felony trial with her.

Stevens seems a little too chummy and I move a step away and put my file innocently between us. I pretend to read what I have memorized and he whispers:

"You're not fooling me, Miss McLeod. You know I read minds, don't you?"

"Don't," I say. "Reading my mind is a threat only when it's actually functioning."

We share a laugh. "I enjoyed dinner last night. The barbecue was good and I liked the jukebox and the ambiance of a real dive. Phyll loved it and my ...". I don't know what to call Jake so I just stop talking. It was a local brewery restaurant where you could eat to the sound of country and western music and go home or stay and dance for a while. I danced with both gentlemen, as did Phyllis, and determined part of Jake's upbringing involved something like Miss Patty's Academy of Dance—he was very good! Stevens, on the other hand, was self-trained but sincere. It would be hard for me to say, which was the better experience. It was something I had not anticipated so there were no pre-event anxieties and Phyll and I both let our hair down. I don't know who was more shocked about that: Me or Phyll.

"What do you want to do on this case?" Stevens asked. It's another family assault, which seems to have become my specialty lately.

"I want you to send him up for life, but I have to ask for Deferred and if you say no, at least get probation so he can go home and do it all over again."

"You think I think you're joking," he says; but he takes the papers I offer and studies them. After a while, he reaches the last report and looks up at me.

"Look. Seriously," I say before he can demand jail time. "The assault was bad. I think it even shocked my client, who has to face, for the first time, that her husband will hit her and he is a bully. The Judge let him out on bond with a no contact order, which means they can only talk if it is something to do with parenting. Your complaining witness, which you permitted me to talk to, tells me he honored it and is doing his best to put on a new face. I asked the Judge and she made him complete 18 weeks of Batterer's Intervention as a condition of bond. Your witness says that people tell her he's a changed man. She will testify for you and she will not try to sugar coat it and I told her she did the right thing. If you go with deferred, he has one prior, fifteen years ago as a Juvie. They have three children. She needs the support and doesn't know if they will get back together. If it's just a show, we'll know real fast and I will send your complaining witness right back here to file charges again if she calls me. You get two shots this way."

He stands there mulling it over.

"Okay, he finally says. I'll recommend it to the Judge. I'm beginning to think she hates these cases, so she might not buy it."

"Will Mrs. Henny?"

"You've done everything right the way she looks at it. She actually likes getting two bites of the apple. It's cheaper on the State too. I'll recommend it and get the papers.

"And, yes," he says as he starts to move away from the corner we have been in to have a semi-private conversation about the plea. "Last night was great and I still have something to talk to you about; but I will use that to get another date after Motherfucker's no longer your shadow."

I look at my watch. I'm early and decide this is a chance to go to my own personal investigation headquarters, the morgue at the offices of the *Enterprise*, which is just across the side street to the Courthouse. I dutifully text Jake to report on where I'm going to be and to tell him where to pick me up and to text when he is outside the building.

One thing about having a quasi-bodyguard, I do not have to drive the Harley to and from work so my appearance is a little neater.

Susan Miller, the records custodian and librarian for the *Enterprise* unlocks the morgue, which stays locked, she says for security of its precious original documents.

I ask for files on David Dickerson. He has expanded into two redwells that are about three inches thick each. I don't have enough time to read them but I flip through every document, turning the ones I want to go back to crosswise in the file without taking them back. If I don't get to read them, I can order copies and pick them up when Ms. Miller has them ready. She is quite helpful and offers to start doing that as soon as she sees me finish one folder. I say thank you and hand it to her and start with the next file.

After looking through both, I lean back disappointed.

I found several profiles on Dickerson but nothing has a reference to his ranch. I'll read them with Phyll later and see if we can improve our guessing about where it is.

Since the small photo in his bathroom is an aerial and since we now know Dickerson has a license to fly and a clean record with the FAA, it makes sense that when he's not carrying camping gear, he flies. The aerial does not show a landing strip or even a grass pasture long and wide enough for a small plane to land on. Our field here started private and became public and due to the traffic is now a regular field. They have no record of him filing a flight plan, which he is supposed to do. So we think he leaves from another field. Using a succession of Phyll's throw downs, we call around to see if he flies out of one of the several private strips between here and Highways 10 and 59 and get no hits.

We check off a field near Interstate10 that has apartments that can be rented and each apartment has its own hanger. I know this place. The owner is a tall, lanky guy with graying hair who runs the place with his daughter. Both fly. We hit pay dirt!

Using one of Phyll's throw downs, I do our usual routine and just ask for the doctor from anybody who answers the phone.

"He's not here." A voice that sounds male and up there in years answers the phone.

"Well he told me he would be there this morning."

A slow-talker with a deep and gravelly voice, the man takes his time; and then says:

"Well, he ain't and I haven't seen him today, or this week, or this month. Maybe he just fed you a line."

His laugh does not make me feel good; but bells are ringing. I know where Dickerson flies out of and why he is not prone to file a flight plan. He just doesn't have to as long as the field is open. He checks in and goes.

"Well, that may be true, Honey," I say, using my best imitation of Phyll, "But he doesn't ever stay away from me that long. Do you have the number out at the ranch?" I say. "I misplaced my little black book."

"Maybe you left it where you shouldn't have been." Again he giggles as if he is the world's funniest comedian. "Let me look for it," he says and I hear drawers being pulled and hear what probably is a call notes pad slammed on his desk.

"Hold on," he barks. "This phone's gonna drive me crazy!"

When he comes back, he says:

"Okay, Darlin', now who'd you say you are again?"

"Now, Honey, you're making me feel real bad. You know me. Miss Babe," Again I use Phyll's voice and get pay dirt.

"Oh, yes, little girl. I'm not gonna forget you for sure. Here's the number and he recites it while I write it down."

"What's that town again? Pretty close. I must have my mind on too many other things I shouldn't be thinking about, you'd say, but I forget it," I say, sounding as helpless as I can be.

"Oh I wish you hadn't asked. Only been there once, had to fly the plane out to get him when he was in a hurry. You remember that, you wuz with him!"

"Sure," I say, "I don't know why my mind's not functioning now."

"Aw, it must be catching. I can't think of that place for the life of me but it's where that guy put concrete ditch liners in the dessert and they call it art. Seen it from the air and up close and it's no big deal."

"Honey you are so nice," I say. "I'll ask for you when I come through again."

"Henry," he says. "Okay Miss Babe you stay as pretty as you are, Honey."

And we hang up in unison.

"Marfa," I tell Phyll. "Middle of nowhere, but it connects by private plane to all of Texas. Long drive though. Do we want to drive it or fly it?"

"We definitely want to fly it," Jake says, coming out of my office, which he has practically taken over and, which I don't complain about as long as he keeps updating my timeline. Phyll lets me use her office, but I spend most of my time at the kitchen table, which is where I often do my real work.

"You shouldn't let me know what a conniving female you are," he says, grinning because he knows I broke the code on Dr. David Dickerson's heretofore unknown ranch. If he flies into Marfa, which has about 1,900 people spread around the desert, someone is sure to either keep his car for him or give transportation to the ranch. My best guess is Goose picks him up and somebody is sure to know how to find a man called Goose.

CHAPTER THIRTY-THREE
Flying /The Real Morgue

Flying is not my favorite thing but Jake tells me he is the best. I don't doubt it, but he senses my need for more than his expert opinion.

"I trained in the United States Marine Corps," he explains, "and they put a lot of high-dollar machines in my care. You are safe and the plane and pilot are free. That's the best part."

I accept his promise, but I don't get to act on it anyway. The phone rings and Phyll tells me it's a call I have to take and comes and stands by my chair. I push away the legal pad I'd been taking notes on and pick up the telephone.

"I'm looking for Felipe Hernandez," the woman's curt voice requests in a very formal manner.

"This is not his number, but I can try to help you."

"Do you know a Shadow McLeod?"

"I do."

"He listed her as next of kin," the woman informs me, again very formally and I start shaking.

"Who is this?" I demand.

"The Harris County Medical Examiner's Office," she says. "I am sorry to shock you, but we have a body that needs to be identified."

I sink into my chair and am unable to hold back the tears.

"Can you help us?"

"Yes, yes, of course. It's just I didn't expect this."

"I do understand," the woman says, softening for the first time.

"Tell me where to come."

"We had a body transported to us from Galveston because we do their autopsies; but before that happens, I'm trying to trace identity. I have to notify the next of kin."

"Of course." Better me than his Mama, I think and I try to pull deep into that resolve that seems close enough to the surface to deal with surprises. This one is devastating.

"The location is not hard to get to but the complex is so big that I need to tell you specifics. Come up Highway 288, if that's convenient," she suggests.

"I can make it so," I say.

"Exit Holcomb and take Exit 81 into the John P. McGovern Medical School complex. Check in with the guard and they'll send you to our location. I will call ahead. Meet me, I'm Elizabeth Scott, and I'll get you there the rest of the way."

"I'll leave as soon as I can," I say. "But it'll probably take me a couple hours."

I look at the phone on my desk and remember the probable tap.

I hang up the phone and look up at Phyll. "I hate to do this to you but I just don't think I can do this alone."

CHAPTER THIRTY-FOUR
The Case of the Lost Body

"Call your boyfriend and see if he knows this already."

"First, he's not my boyfriend—I'm a little old for that. Friend. Possible interest."

"Well, you know who I'm talking about."

"Rand. Just call him Rand."

"Yes Ma'am," I agree. "Call Rand and ask him why they said it was a woman's body at Babe's house when Fee Lo is the one in the morgue?"

"I already did that while you were on the phone. He swears that's what they said. He never saw it, the body, but he says everyone would have known, and it would have blown the lid off the courthouse had it been Fee Lo."

"Doesn't make sense," I agree. "Did he promise not to say anything?"

"Of course, he feels like he's in such deep dodo now with helping the two of us that he's not gonna say even that he's heard of our names, if somebody asks him."

"I'll bet Jake will," I say with a smile trying to cover up for the fact that my breathing is irregular and I am about to scream out in panic. He steps back with his hands in a surrender pose.

"Say he knows us, that is."

"What's happening?"

"You work pretty fast," Phyll says. "She is as skitteresh as a prom queen."

I know she is trying to calm me down by making me angry.

"US big girls require that the going up be worth the coming down," she adds and I realize she is saying enjoy life while it lasts.

"Well guys, thanks for trying, but there is no way we can put this off. Can we take your car, Phyll?"

"Enroute to Houston I am wound up and cannot sit still. I also can't stop talking and realize the gentleman sitting behind me with his hat pulled low on his face is seeing me at my most vulnerable.

"Remember last Summer when I re-read Faulkner?" I ask.

"Vaguely, your reading habits are not my first priority." She is still trying to dig in and I know she's trying to anger me enough to get my verve back.

"I know. I just want to keep talking."

"Understand."

"I read Faulkner in school and never felt like I understood him at all. Read him again when I was teaching that class. You know, History and Government at that Junior College while I worked on a History PhD. I had an office mate, who was an expert on Faulkner, and I re-read him with her. It was like Faulkner's College of One with his Mistress; but Miss Mary walked me through every volume. She was amazing, remembered verbatim quotes from every one of them and explained them like she'd written them herself. Loved Faulkner, she said, because he understood the difference between old money, family, heritage, and new money. No sense of noblesse oblige, he said, and she said his Snopes family was an indictment of everything she detested about New Money in the South, with capital letters."

"Well. She sounds like your typical Southern snob. Probably talked about the Plantation."

"Just the oil on it," I concede. "She was talking about my family," I say. "I knew it, but just denied it at the time. Then when I read Faulkner again this Summer to deal properly with Harry as much as anything, I realized just how much her commentary and the Snopes had been an indictment of my family. She hated the bunch of them and didn't even know them."

"I don't give snobs like that the time of day," Phyllis says.

"She wasn't really a total snob. There was a side of her I loved so much because she was doing her best to live life after much of the reason for it was gone. She was old and people no longer liked to be around her because she could be such a bitch. But she had thrived in life. Was an unclaimed jewel, she said, but she'd been claimed more than once. I knew there was a man in her past, who played piano while she sang sultry blues songs, in Puerto Rico, while she worked on a master's degree at the University there, for some reason. I think she might have followed him there to tell the truth."

"What happened?"

"She said she gave him up due to his marriage. I think it might have been the other way around. When she struck out for her freedom from him, she packed up lock, stock, and barrel and took passage on a slow-moving cargo steamer home. Very romantic. Just the thing a tall, thin, willowy, gravel-throated blonde would have looked great doing. Right out of the movies. I pictured Lauren Bacall playing her role. She landed at New Orleans. Said she couldn't believe the irony. Landing there.

Brass bands were playing.

"What's going on," she had asked the only steward who had taken care of the five or six paying passengers on the cargo ship.

"Funeral," he says. "Funeral for Delilah Orchid."

"Who?" She had asked.

"The most famous Madame in New Orleans," the steward said, dragging it out.

"Was she older to have so many friends?" The wharf had been packed with people and the band played loud and strong and erotically when a saxophone joined in.

"She was young," he answered. "Most beautiful woman New Orleans ever saw. A passionate Puerto Rican. Dark, beautiful black eyes and hair to the waist. Sang like a nightingale under the influence of the moon. Her voice was low and husky," he remembered.

He wiped a tear.

"'My, my,'" Mary said that she had said, and held him around the shoulders.

"He killed her. Young man also from Puerto Rico sliced that beautiful throat so it could never sing again. Could not take that other men loved her too and that she loved them back."

"Mary said it left an indelible impression she would write about. There she was, Mary the future English teacher, an aging songstress herself, getting off a slow cargo ship making her way back home because she was giving up on love and leaving Puerto Rico to get away from the passion. And here was this young woman, who let her passion lead her to the streets, and who had the ability to make grown men cry for her, going home to Puerto Rico on Mary's same ship in a coffin.

"Later, Mary said, she watched them bring her casket to the landing plank before they brought Mary's luggage off. But she never took the time to write about it. I thought she couldn't say what she wanted to say because that community was so conservative. She probably would have lost her job."

"I would like to have read it," Phyllis says. "She sounds real after all!"

"I agree. The young just should not die." My body shakes and I know that I am filling the car with sobs.

"I know, I know, I know." Phyllis says, patting me on the knee.

We are at our destination; and I take a yellow button from the access machine and find a parking place for Visitors and sit there letting the tears flow until I feel somewhat empty.

"You ready?" Phyllis says after a while.

"No, but I don't think we have a choice."

We follow Elizabeth Scott's directions, pass through an art school she later explained was renting space, and found her to be a lot nicer than she sounded on the phone.

"I'll go with you so we can talk on the way."

As usual, she gives her attention to Jake as if Phyll and I are not there or are invisible. I suspect the latter is true. She is short, heavy set, and somewhat strident in her walk and mannerisms. She leads Jake into a locked section of the massive complex and checks us in. We sit and wait and ultimately a young man wearing doctor's scrubs comes for us. His white mask is over his forehead but before he leads us to the back, again, leading Jake and letting Phyll and me follow, he hands Jake three masks and Jake dutifully passes one to each of us. He tells us to put it on as he hands each of us a similar mask and I note the authority in his voice.

"Don't let this go to your head," I tell him.

The Assistant Medical Examiner lowers his voice as we walk into the empty room, which is about five degrees colder than is comfortable.

"It might be uncomfortable," he says, "but we have to keep it this cold or the smell sometimes is too bad for people from the outside."

"Let's see." He studies the sheet Elizabeth Scott gives him. "Poor thing," he says, shaking his head and motioning us to the side of a room that seems all stainless steel. I can't help thinking that Fee Lo would object to being called "Poor Thing" and I resent it for him and cannot help the tears that run behind my mask and down my cheek and puddle at the end of my chin before dropping off. A microphone is suspended from the ceiling and a pretty deep drain sits approximately where I expected a gurney to come to rest. He leaves us and comes back with what we expected.

"But this is not what we expected," he says. "We had every reason to expect this to be Lorena . . ."

"What," I say, interrupting. "Lorena?"

"Lorena," he says.

"A woman?" I ask. "I was called to come up here because I was next of kin to Fee Lo? Felipe Hernandez."

"I don't know a Fee Lo. No one by that name is here."

Phyllis grabs my shoulders and pulls me close. She is as relieved as I am.

"Are you two gonna be okay doing this?" he asks, not comprehending what is happening.

We nod silently and he pulls back the sheet.

"Her editor came up but he said this is not Lorena. She was found in property they identified as Lorena's house. We called you because you were the only contact for the male they said was her friend."

"Her editor is correct," I say. "The name of this woman is Sharon Rose Donaldson."

"Why does that sound familiar?" he asks.

"It was she who reported both Lorena—Babe—and Fee Lo, Felipe Hernandez, missing from Rutter Industries. She was the Human Resources Manager at that company. I guess she learned too much," I say as his eyes grow wide. I look closely at Sharon Rose Donaldson, whose face is serene, as if a burden has lifted.

"Can you tell the cause of death?" I ask.

"Suffocation is pretty obvious in this case. She is young and healthy. But I'm not allowed to tell you the cause at this time." Jake actually pulls Elizabeth Scott aside and I do not hear their conversation; but she tells the attending doctor:

"You can release the autopsy report to the gentleman."

So there.

Jake reaches out and touches the gurney. I don't learn until the trip back to the office that he had made contact with Sharon Donaldson after we met in Dallas and she dutifully started giving them information until she disappeared. Phyll and I had looked for her and had even gone out to her Mother's house to check on her whereabouts to no avail. All her Mother knew was that the nice man came around to tell her that Sharon got a promotion and had to go on a big trip for Rutter, her employer. She knew Sharon would be gone for several days. What we did not have the nerve to tell her yet was that Sharon would not be coming back.

Phyll, true to her pledge, visited the Mother at least every other day while we also looked for Sharon.

We don't know what Jake and his superiors did and they never said.

CHAPTER THIRTY-FIVE
Ben Ramsey is Back

"Jake," I tell him when we are alone. "I have the distinct impression you are leading me down the primrose path for your boss, but I need a friend right now. The pressure from this is getting to me. That girl was such a precious human being. She just should not have died that way without making somebody pay."

"We will," he says. "One way or another we generally end up doing justice." He puts his arms around me, but I try to pull away. He correctly assessed that talking is probably not everything that I need, but I am truly not looking for that from him.

"I have to do this all the time," he tells me. "And it never gets any easier."

"She was a fountain of information that will help us make that case if we can get them just before they act," Jake says. "She gave us their deadline, which is right now." Jake put his hand on my shoulder. "She had no idea what they were doing, but she sent your friend Fee Lo into the East Field, and he tried to keep her informed about what he was finding. Waiting and getting them after they start is crucial to making the conspiracy claim, and we can do it now. Sharon Rose Donaldson loved being an FBI confidential informant. She loved working with Fee Lo. She jumped right into it. She told me and Fee Lo it was the greatest feeling she ever had, knowing that she was fighting back against McNelly. I'm afraid now that it made her feel invincible, like nothing could ever hurt her."

"It hurts," I say.

"She had to stay on the job, but that made it easier. I don't know how he found out unless she told him; but Jack McNelly's hand is all over her death and we will get him."

He drains the coffee we'd made earlier.

"I have to let you know something else," he says. "We met when

I fished you out of the water when Ben Ramsey tried to take you to paradise with him. You would have found out ultimately but the reason I'm here with you is that Ben Ramsey is back on the scene."

"Ben Ramsey is dead," I say. "I was there. He could not have survived falling into the props."

"Maybe not," Jake concedes, "but his fingerprints did. His prints were picked up at Babe's house and our theory is that he killed Sharon somewhere else but brought her there to dump her body."

He puts his arms around me and pulls me close. Neither of us is in a romantic mood, but it is obvious we both need another human being that is alive and can return a touch. He puts his hands on my shoulders, as he often does when he is just telling me nothing. The time of day. I don't know him well enough to know if its kindness or control talking.

"Alexandra McLeod, I love you. I love you with all my heart. I want to spend every day of my life with you until our time is over on this earth and then I want to be with you through eternity. When my last molecule makes its way free and hits the very end of the universe, I want to be so close to you it combines with your last molecule."

I can't control the tears. "Please don't say things like that," I say.

He kisses me in a way I've never been kissed. He is good but that is off the wall wonderful!

"Let's go walk on the beach," he says. "And then lets make love the rest of the evening and maybe into the morning and afternoon for about the next ten days with our phones off," he says as his starts to ring, "and without telling anyone where we are."

And we did make it to the beach.

"I don't think your friend is missing," Jake says as we stroll along the deserted beach. "I think he's become a mole in that section of Rutter to find out what's going on. I will protect him. Or I will try; but you know he's a little bit like a real mole—he slips away like magic."

He picks up a shell and throws it out into the surf the way you would do if you skipped rock as Texas men think they have to do or you will think their manhood is slipping. He throws with expert skill but it doesn't skip and he grins self-consciously.

"You must have a reason," I say.

"Just a suspicion," he replies. He says nothing for a while as we continue our walk into the State Park's territory and then further on to the next subdivision. "Ever wish there was no one else around but you and the birds and whatever's out there in the water?"

"Not lately," I say. "Things have been too messy lately to want to be alone."

"I mean if times weren't messy, as you say."

"If they weren't messy and it was somebody like you and me, I can imagine wanting everybody else in the world to be out of our way."

He puts an arm around me, then brushes off the sand he inadvertently got on my shoulder.

"The one and only time I had to call 911 out here," I say. "The fireplace fell in. Everything corrodes overnight and the builder was supposed to have put in a new one after Ike but I think he may only have thought he did when he billed for it. Lit a fire and the metal chimney came tumbling into the firebox. I dialed 911 and the operator said. 'Well, Ma'am how do you expect me to know where you are when I'm in La Marque and you're not?'"

"I just called 911," I say.

"I know you did; but the Galveston Sheriff forwards the calls to me at night. They gotta shortage or something going on."

"Just give the fire department a buzz," I say. "I feel like I ought to go outside since that's what they tell you to do if you get a fire."

"I can try it," she says. "I'm not sure I can explain to them where you are."

"They came, I guess, since your house is still standing," he says.

"Oh, yes," I say. "Fire never left the fireplace box but it sure looked like it might."

He stops and bends over to pick up another shell, starts to throw it and stops.

"You know you're really good looking, don't you?"

"Sometimes," I admit. "Most times not."

"Do you remember cross examining me during a trial before Judge Lew where you tricked me into giving up my confidential informant?"

"Was that you?" I start but don't pursue the façade. "Of course I remember!"

"I hoped you wouldn't. You were so intense and so mad at me

because you couldn't trick me into letting on who it was so you gave me his name and said do you deny that. I just gave it up to avoid lying under oath."

"You Bastard," I say, kicking the sand with the open toe of my old salt-water-laden tennis shoe that is worn away from age. "It did make me mad."

"Don't say that," he says, laughing. "I thought you were so cute I gave it away just to please you. You actually finally asked the question where I had to answer or lie and not even the Feds require me to lie under oath.

'That's why I served those papers on you that day. I just wanted to see you up close again. It hit me hard when you were brow-beating me. No woman has ever treated me that way and I wanted to cry like a little boy. Prosecutor thought I was playing you to get where he knew I wanted to go. Said he saw what happened out there and I'd better watch out if I was that soft for a pretty face."

"And are you?" I ask.

"Only where you're concerned, apparently," he says and throws the shell. It almost skips, which is damn near impossible in surf.

"I'll bet you tell every woman that," I say laughing.

"Only redheads," he admits. Stops. Puts his arms around me and shows me just how practiced he is at peeling away resistance.

It is so nice seeing an end to a long dry spell on the horizon, but once more it is not to be.

"What on earth?" he asks as we open the gate to get onto the deck of my house. Something was dropped inside the gate and dragged against the deck as he opened the gate. He started to pick it up before moving it to the side and opening the gate. "I got something in my trunk to handle this," he says. "I think we ought to x-ray it," he says. "Before we play with it too much. It doesn't feel right to me. Heavier than it should be."

He is down the stairs and back up in a flash, holding a metal canister into which he slides the small package and closes the seal. He walks more carefully going down the stairs and puts the canister in his trunk.

"You can go or you can stay," he says. "Either way, we're not finished."

We were.

Neither of us had any way of knowing the night was ruined for romance. There would be no ten days of running away from the package, which contained a gun.

He x-rayed and opened it in the crime lab at the federal building and had the technician check it for prints. It was wiped clean, except for one print, which was no surprise, but Rand's missing service revolver was now in an evidence locker at the federal courthouse. And Fee Lo's thumbprint was carefully pressed onto the handle in a way he could not have put it there during use and was quickly identified by the FBI's computerized search service.

"The good thing," Jake says. "It suggests that your buddy is still out there somewhere, sometime after that woman was shot and killed with Rand's service revolver. I'm betting he put the print there himself because it sure is carefully placed to refute his ever doing so while shooting it."

He pulled out his cell and I figured out that it was Rand when he started telling him what had been so unceremoniously delivered to us. As they talk, he reaches out and takes my hand and pulls it into a fairly nice warm spot between his arm and his shirt.

CHAPTER THIRTY-SIX
Phyll Takes a Fall

"Okay!" Phyll says, total disgust in her voice. "Look at my new $110. dollar leggings from Lemon Yellow! Every time I get a new pair, I have another disaster hit!" The leggings are torn down one side, her elbow and arm are bleeding, hair is all over the place, and her composure is faltering.

"That is the last time you'll push that f-ing Harley off on me. It rolled over on me at the intersection. Just as I was looking pretty good on it to a guy in a Corvette."

"We don't date Corvette guys anyway," I say. I had already run to her at the door, but she brushed me off, and pushed me away.

No pity is the rule.

Notwithstanding, I make the lawyer's typical plea: "Honey I am so sorry that happened to you. You looked so good on it too!"

"Whuhf," she blows out breath. "Humph. Oh my pride is so hurt. These leggings are so expensive."

"We'll replace them from petty cash," I suggest. "See if you have enough in there. You were on duty at the time. Isn't it great about Fee Lo, though?"

"Only if he gets his ass back here and gives us back your car!"

"Okay, you're right about that. And it's speculation that he's all right somewhere and is not in a position to call in and tell us what's going on."

"Tell me what happened with Jake."

"J. Edgar? That's his real name I discovered. It's too good not to use. No. That's privileged!"

"No, Girl-Who-Never-Opens-Her-Mouth-About-The-Real-Stuff. Not about the sex, which will probably be better the way I imagine it than what you'll admit to anyway. Tell me everything that happened from the time you picked up the package."

"Well, if it came from Fee Lo, and I can only hope," he left it on the deck at the house when J. Edgar and I were walking, on the beach in fairly romantic circumstances. He's a talker. He's also a pretty good listener."

I tell her as much as I can remember. The landline rings and Phyllis picks it up: "Shadow McLeod and Associates."

Pause.

"She's here. May I tell her who's calling?"

Pause. She watches the number on the call notes disappear.

Quickly dials the two-digit number that shows the number again. Writes it down.

"It wasn't Fee Lo," she says. "He wanted to know if you appreciated the gift he left you on your deck."

"Who was he?"

"I don't know, I'm trying to get this number to ring back but it won't. Maybe somebody else uses prepaids as throw down phones. My guess is it's the same guy who waited for us at Babe's and tried to take out Rand."

I get up and leave the room. The heavy feeling descends on me once more. Somebody has Fee Lo and my guess is that it is somebody at Rutter or for Rutter.

"Pull up that Rutter Application Form off the Internet and let's both go looking for a job."

"Not on your life," Phyllis says. "That place is deadly to me."

"We're not ever going to work there, Child. We're just going to see what kind of reception we get from Sharon Rose Donaldson."

"You know she's dead," Phyllis says as if shocked that I have lost my marbles.

"They don't know that we know that. Do you still have that cute little blonde/brown wig you wore to the Mardi Gras Party at the Fremont last year?"

"Of course, it costs too much to get rid of and I figured it was inevitable that I might need to go incognito for you somewhere else."

"Go home and put on your best Baptist-Sunday-Looking flower printed dress and wear that wig. I'm gonna call both of our friends to see which one, if either, can give you backup that doesn't look hunkish, but who can beat the shit out of Jack McNelly if he gets half an excuse."

"Sounds like a plan. I guess it has to be me if we're gonna be anonymous."

"You're also more clever than I am you know."

"Sneakier," she agrees.

"I want you to get something off this guy if he shows up. DNA maybe...".

"No f-ing way. What do you think I am?"

"Not that way silly. There's more than one source for DNA. If you can't charm him into a drink or coffee so you can steal the cup, scratch the hell out of him and protect that hand with gloves. You'll come up with something better than that anyway. Put on your best Sunday School Teacher Act. You had an appointment this afternoon with Sharon Donaldson and you are going to show up for it in full secretarial array with Application in hand, including a mission statement about your work in Middle America saving orphans on one of Rutter's own projects for the poor there. You taught at the Jesus School Rutter helped you finance and did so every summer till you graduated College. You can blow this one away. I see Oscar potentiality. You go get dressed and I will type up the Application and your mission statement. What happened to that camera we used in Bobby Gene's case to catch Imogene taking the cash money home tucked in her extremely exaggerated bosoms?"

"It's in the storage room, I think. You know that was another fun night out if you recall. It's called letting your hair down now and then, which I've now seen you do exactly twice in how many ... can it be eight years by now?""

"Oh, I recall all right. I just wouldn't want to have to do that case over for love nor money. Not that it helped us in the case anyway since Bobby Gene's personal Judge kept it out."

"I sure would like to have a picture of this guy," I add. I'm betting this Jack McNelly's got a story and is on somebody's watch list."

"Maybe J. Edgar can id him since we're pretty sure that name is a first-class fake." I add, liking the idea of getting a picture of this guy."

"And a kinda stupid one at that," Phyllis throws in.

"I just want one quick look at a man stupid enough to take on a pseudonym of two venerated Texas Rangers! He's either got nothing between his ears or something more than an elbow up his sleeve. And he is mean," I say.

"We know that. And a stupid M-F who doesn't deserve to live," Phyllis says, copying my best friend, who often calls just to say another lawyer has moved into her privileged group of lawyers who don't deserve to live.

And, of course, Mr. Badguy is there when Phyllis makes her appearance timely for her appointment with Human Resources. Ms. Donaldson is away on vacation, he explains, but he has volunteered to take her calendar. He apologizes for not finding Cynthia Freeman's name and appointment on Donaldson's calendar, or he would have done the decent thing and called her to cancel. But he is happy for the chance to meet her and tell her how great life is for those working at Rutter.

And, of course, Rand, who is becoming very protective of our Little Precious One, brought out a blood brother, sworn to protect her with his life, to accompany this very demure little Sunday School worker, who needs to get a job to support the family since Sweet Wonderful Harry, her long-time husband, who is a decade or two older than she, has had a bad accident and is out of work, maybe permanently, and unable to help out due to his bad back. I hear, after the fact, that Harry, whom we affectionately named after my dear departed Asshole Ex, is the meanest mother you could hope to find at the gym where they worship a militant T'ai Quan Do and break boards and concrete blocks with their bare hands in their down time. Given the reception we think this guy gave Rand, Harry, Chin his real name, promises to treat Bad Guy's neck to a sample of his own punishment.

And of course, Phyllis knows better than to suggest a drink to this Mr. Badguy, since she is a true Baptist Sunday School worker, and, true to form, one of them, Chin I think, got Badguy's picture in natural color while Phyllis is practicing her wiles and finds a way to trip herself and fall all over him in the process of delivering the Application she has prepared for Ms. Donaldson, who was just wonderful when she talked to her.

"God-Damn!" he starts out with an expletive, as Phyllis' little pinkie digs into the tender skin inside his wrist and damn near bleeds him out, a wound she kindly soaks with a Kleenex she just happens to have handy, which she stuffs into a Ziplock bag she just happens to have hidden in her purse waiting. And poor Harry/Chin, bad back and all, is all over Badguy's ass in a second, bad back and all, because Chin is unprepared for drama that involves His Phyllis' having physical injury. And, since he thinks all the blood came from her, he stops only briefly as Badguy apologizes.

"My Goodness, Girl," Badguy corrects his attitude in deference to the Sunday School teacher; but it is too late to soothe over Harry/ Chin's enormous protective attitude for his supportive little wife. "Little man, don't you worry. I never hit a woman in my life!" Attempting to laugh, Badguy lets Phyllis scrub away the bloody residue from the scratch that goes down his wrist to his finger.

"Oh, my Goodness. I guess I'll never get a job here now," she wails as he pats her on the back with his good hand.

And, of course, with photograph and DNA sample in hand, the two of them make their apologies and back out of the office.

"I'll have Ms. Donaldson call you, Young Lady, when she gets back from her trip."

"Well, for sure," I say, after hearing all of this and giving J. Edgar what we hoped would be enough of a DNA sample.

"I could start a business with this," he says appreciatively of the amount and isolation of the sample.

"I don't think that's a very positive response from him, frankly Phyll, since we know poor Sharon Donaldson is not coming back from the vacation trip he gave her."

"I risked my life, this time," Phyll says. "But my little old Asian husband is as outstanding as they say!" She giggles. "He is quick on his feet for sure, when he thought I was really hurt. I didn't want to spoil the effect for him by telling him about it in advance."

"You and every man you come in contact with," I say, shaking my head. For a woman with an ass that causes heads to turn for second glances, Phyll keeps a line out the door when she is open for business. "I'm almost sorry he didn't get to knock the guy out. Just for grins."

"Oh, but he did," Phyllis corrects me, laughing. "Badguy made the mistake of asking Harry/Chin just what kind of chink he is to learn to fight that way and that little monster took offense. He picked up this huge fella, swung him over his head. Brought him down to earth on his head. And sealed things with a karate chop to the neck that I'll bet won't straighten itself out for months. He apologized profusely the whole time he was doing it and bowed several times for the discourtesy, saying all the while: 'No man touches my Little Precious! Chin is certifiably committable."

"That's not a word," I say.

"You know what I mean, Smartass," she answers, squinting beedy little eyes in my direction and adds: "I'm rethinking those mild little Asian men roaming around here. I'll warn Rand to never cross him."

And you guessed it. Over the course of a twenty-minute relationship, Phyllis acquires yet another new man to protect her, who is so overly possessive of her safety, Ryan has to send him on jobs to have time with Phyllis for himself. If we could only bottle her appeal and market it, none of us would ever have to worry again about paying the rent.

Chapter Thirty-seven
Fee Lo Pays Another Visit

Things were just beginning to settle back into normal when Fee Lo actually calls.

"Can't talk," he says. "Come get me at the same place, the same way. He hangs up the phone and I glance quickly at the clock while pulling on the same jeans I had dropped on the floor at bedtime. I am dog tired because I was up late getting ready for a hearing on a Motion to Quash a Deposition on a case at 8 tomorrow morning before the Judge goes back into trial on another case. I noticed the Deposition because I thought the little skank, who is the under-aged Defendant in my case, will try to lie his way out of the story I know to be supported by a credible witness, a teacher who was also at the same event when Hank the Hunk threw a football, playfully of course, at my girl and broke out her two front teeth, which is not fun to a 16 year old girl who'd turned him down for a date. The Defense Lawyer, who is just doing his job, Noticed my Client after he got my Notice of Deposition, but he wanted to push up the Deposition of my client to a couple days before his client's. I knew he was suspicious that his kid is a lying-piece-of-you-know-what; and I wasn't sure I even wanted to do the Motion to Quash his deposition until after mine, but I feared that if I didn't, he'd just allow his boy to match his story to my girl's with just enough innocence added to avoid liability. I know that I know things that he doesn't at this point. I am trying to figure out how to tell the Judge without telling the Judge that it is part of strategy.

Fee Lo's voice blows my head clear and I am out the door with the Harley key before two minutes have passed. I head West on Highway 3005 and then turn on 8 mile Road to hit Stewart. The East Field in the Rutter Complex hugs the Bay and is fenced and is well-lit this time. It takes me a good thirty minutes. No opening seems readily available in the fence and I slowly circle trying to keep the sound of the Harley as low as I can but that's impossible if you've ever driven one and I'm not the expert. I spot a new passageway and half expect to see Fee Lo in the opening; but I slip through it and am beside the second stack in short measure. Still no Fee Lo. Then I see him. Standing on the edge, I can tell he is blind-folded and a fella as big as the one I imagined from the lump on Rand's head is standing over him and about to push.

"Miss Mcloud," he calls out. I know it is Badguy; but I also know now that J. Edgar ran him on the databases and is getting ready for him. I know how stupid I was for coming out here without calling Rand or Jake to give me help.

"Fee Lo are you okay?"

"They made me call you," he says. "I wish you hadn't listened to me."

"They knew I would," I call back up to him.

"Look out! Shadow. He's got somebody down there with you. He wants to talk."

"I don't want to talk to him," I say. I start up the bike and see a thug about as big at the one on the rack with Fee Lo headed toward me. I don't know where he came from; but I know the best defense against a bully is a good offense.

"Jump!" I order, hoping Fee Lo remembers what he did last time. "I can get you out of here!"

"It's hard to grab a rope, when they've got your hands tied. Get out of here now, while you can!"

The big oaf approaches the bike in a run and I rev it, leaving what I hope is at least a bruise across his back. I hear his expletive as he rolls away from the bike and into the rocks on the path; but I am feeling no pain by now and adrenaline is coursing through me in a way I never knew I was capable of and I am willing and ready to kill this bastard as I swing the bike around just as he starts lifting himself from the ground. I head for him as forcefully as I can; but, I veer the bike away from him and slow beneath the rack just as Fee Lo's body hits the dirt. I turn the bike to get between him and the hulk and he crawls on the back and hangs on to me like no human being ever has before. The shot pops and misses just as Fee Lo frees his hands and takes over the bike.

"Never have two arms felt so damned good," I tell him.

"I would have shot that bastard myself if I had had my gun," he grunts.

"No shit!" I exclaim as the two of us hunker down to get back out of the fence. Badguy is still on top of the rack and I expect him to give one last shot but he doesn't. As best we could tell, he is directing his fire below us at his own henchman on the ground. We hear his companion protest and then take off in a run.

When we get to my office, Fee Lo and I hold each other for a long, long time, both of us still shaking from the experience.

"I can't live without you," I tell him. "You're the closest thing to real family that I've ever had. I love you, you little bastard; and this has been the most awful month and a half of my life. Not knowing what happened to you and feeling danger everywhere without you—it was just horrible. And they killed Sharon Donaldson and she just didn't deserve that and you're always gonna be my best friend. You're my brother. You're essential to me And I agree with your Mother: You've got to stop jumping off buildings and ...."

"Okay, okay, everything is okay now. I'm through out there! He holds me tight again and starts laughing, arching his eyebrows into a frown. He pushes me back and looks at me long and hard.

"Is that all you can say?" he demands. "I was ready to lay down my life for you and you're my best friend is what I get?"

"Well, what more can I give you, Fee Lo; it's like your Mama sent you to me and told me I have to take care of you because you sure don't mind her. I know you love Babe and all those other women. You're too good a friend to waste on sex!"

He starts laughing.

Then I start laughing.

Then we both laugh together and then Jake walks into the room as if he's been there waiting the entire time and has heard everything.

Then he starts laughing.

It is the first time I'd heard laughs like that and it seems to be just a huge sigh of relief.

But Jake says:

"Shadow McLeod and Felipe Hernandez, you are both under arrest. You have the right to remain silent. Anything that you do say may be used against you in a court of law. You have the right to have a lawyer present during any questioning by the police or representatives of the government. If you cannot afford to hire a lawyer, one will be appointed to represent you." He looks at Felipe. "If you are not a citizen of this country…" he starts, but Fee Lo interrupts.

"I don't need this. Man, what is this shit? I was born here same as you!"

"…You have the right to ask me to notify your embassy," Jake completed the Miranda warning.

"Jake," I say. "What on earth is going on?"

Needless to say, as a lawyer, I'm a little unglued by a Miranda recitation directed at me.

"They filed charges against the two of you. I asked the feds to let me bring you in. Rutter Industries has filed theft of intellectual property charges against you both. They say the property is federal and licensed to the military and that makes it a federal crime, along with criminal trespass, breaking and entering and destroying a fence on property where top secret projects take place. And they have told us that they have evidence that implicates Felipe Hernandez in the disappearance of one Lorena Burnet and in the murder of Sharon Rose Donaldson."

"That's impossible," I say."First, I am his lawyer. I am licensed by the State of Texas and I am a lawyer until the Supreme Court of the State of Texas takes that license away. I know there can't be an indictment yet—that comes from the Grand Jury. Fee Lo, I instruct you to make no statements. Do not talk to me here in the presence of this officer, and do not talk to me over any phone in our immediate area. I will tell you when we are some place that it is safe to talk."

"Shadow, listen to me, Sweetheart!"

Fee Lo raises his eyebrows. "Sweetheart?" he says. "You can't stoop that low, Shadow."

"Don't worry about that," I say. "He's not who I thought he was. Jake, you don't have time to do all the explaining you're gonna have to do after this. Rutter Industries is up to something. I don't know what it is; but it's dangerous and it can't be good for the world when they try this hard to protect knowledge about it. I went and identified that poor little woman they killed off for I don't know what reason; but she was actually a nice person. Fee Lo could not have done that because of a series of events I have documented, including those you are part of. When I rescued him tonight, two of the biggest thugs I've ever seen were out there and one of them tried to get to me and did shoot at us and the other one pushed Fee Lo off the rack. It could have killed him. The only reason the two of us even made it away is pure and simple mystery. It ain't our time to go, I 'spect." I stop and draw in a deep breath. "Boy are you a major disappointment."

He shakes his head.

"I am not high enough up to tell you what you'll come to know and understand. I was out there tonight. I knew when he called you because I was listening in on the call. They forced him to do it. Said get you out there or they would send somebody to your house and make him watch them while they hurt you. It was the right thing, him calling you.

"There is something going on out there and we have a suspicion some high mucky mucks know about it and are helping Rutter keep it closed off from even us. I can tell you I think their bouncer comes with a long history and we don't have the DNA matches yet because you know it takes longer for that; but we know who he is. If he had known how close he is to getting cover and identity blown, he might have jumped himself rather than pushed Fee Lo off the rack."

"He didn't pay attention the first time we did that move," I say. "Fee Lo was able to grab the rope just in time to break his fall."

"Phyllis got a pretty good fingerprint on that application she handed to him and backed out of that office with a coffee cup that had another one. He's gonna be easy to take down; but we can't do it yet. We believe that in a matter of days, what they're working on will be finished and ready for shipment and it is essential that we find out what they are going to do with it and catch them at that stage or it will be deny, deny, deny; and all traces will disappear.

"This has international implications. The only way I can keep you and your friend here safe and away from them is to lock you up.

"In jail?" I demand.

"I like to call it protective custody. Mine."

"Bullshit!" I was never this mad, even at Harry and he was as insufferable as he was at the end.

"Will you listen to me for five minutes?"

"No, we've done all right so far taking care of ourselves. I guess we can do it a little while longer."

"Shadow." His voice is pleading.

"It's too much to absorb," I tell him. "I'm really short on loyalty to someone who reads me my rights."

"I have to do that," he says with strained patience. "You of all people know that. I wanted to tell you long before now, but I don't belong to me. I've got a boss giving me orders. The only reason that guy didn't shoot ya'll tonight is because he couldn't think fast enough to figure out how to do it there and keep it off Rutter. He's coming to get you. And he will do it. He's brutal. He's sadistic. He works for people who will go down and dirty with our worst enemy; and we are gonna take them down with your help.

"He is getting suspicious that he's got to get on the run and they will track him down and do to him what they did to Lorena and that guy that tried to stop you tonight. They shot him. And that guy's body will disappear without anybody saying prayers over him or coming to look for him. Sharon Rose Donaldson might be a real problem for them. She's got a Mother, who depended on her.

"I cannot let that happen to you. I've waited a long time and I am just not going to let you get away. And after that heartfelt opening of your soul to this guy, I realize I'm getting two of you rather than just one. If I let anything happen to him, I can write you off too. Right?"

Fee Lo is sizing up both of us and starts grinning.

"You sure got busy without my supervision," Fee Lo says to me. "This guy's got it bad and it looks like it's not a one-way street either. Okay, Motheroos," Fee Lo says, turning toward Jake. "Okay, J. Edgar, if that's your name, conveniently the same as one of the most evil men ever to serve in law enforcement, let's go downtown or wherever it is you're keeping us. I'm so damn tired, I just need a shower or a place to stretch out."

"She's got a bed back there," Jake says and smiles. Fee Lo shakes his head in exasperation. "Son-uv-a-bitch, It's just because you're tall," he says to Jake and starts to close the door.

"Uh, leave that door open," Jake says. "I gotta keep an eye on you even when you sleep. I got some guys coming over in a little bit. They had to clean up and get some equipment. Phyllis will be here in about thirty minutes when they pick her up. Rand volunteered. And some little guy who calls himself Harry/Chin will be here. You're gonna be surrounded, but at least you'll have Phyllis to help absorb the testosterone. It's the best I can do, because I can't even assume you're safe in my jail until we bring this guy in and we can't do that until we give them enough rope to hang themselves."

"I'm gonna lie down with him" I say. "I've got a hearing at 8 in the morning."

"I'll be here," he says. "I'm gonna be your shadow for the next ten days. By then you'll know for sure that I really am the best thing that ever happened to you." He puts his arms around me and pulls me close. I am still so angry at him that I try to move away, but his arms hold me tight. It feels good. When he tries to kiss me, I make an effort to resist.

"You can't get away from me," he says.

This time I can't move away from him.

"Leave the door open," he whispers and smiles.

CHAPTER THIRTY-EIGHT
A Motion Gets Caught in Traffic

Judge Lilly Pruser looks at me and must have been overcome by the enormous circles under my eyes.

"You look like shit," she whispers in a most judicial tone.

"All-nighter, Judge."

"Well I hope it was fun. I see your big boy back there keeping watch. I had an anonymous call this morning."

"Don't know about that Judge, but I wouldn't put much stock in people that don't identify themselves."

"Jay Lewis," the Judge calls again. It is now 15 after eight and the other attorney still has not appeared. She looks at me.

"It's your Motion," she says.

"I can pass it Judge; but I sure don't want to. This is important."

"Okay, stay here. I'm gonna get my coffee and if he's not here by 8:30, I'm bringing in my jury, but I'll grant your Motion first."

And, that's what happened.

. . .

Jay Lewis called me later and asked please, because he said he was caught in a butt-load of traffic at "Broadway and 61st and almost abandoned his car to walk the rest of the way to 59th Street, but knew he could try to talk me out of it instead.

"I know you're a good guy," I say. "But a girl's gotta do what a girl's gotta do."

He laughs. "Okay. I guess it'll all come out in the wash as my Dear Sainted Mother used to say. Maybe it'll make sense someday."

Rand and Harry/Chin are dutifully behind me when we get back to my fortified office. Shutters all drawn, plain clothes people just casually cut the grass next door, beat up cars that have to be unmarked cop cars, make my office look like a fire sale is going on at a Land

Office in Oil Country. I wonder if there is that much security at the airports in Houston or Dallas.

"If you plan a shoot-out here," I say. "Would you at least give me some warning and let me just go home."

"Nothing's going to happen here, I promise," he says. "This is a good chance to train."

"So I'm protected by all the Rookies?" I ask.

"Something like that."

I turn to Rand and Chin, who are leaving their own very noticeable marked cars right in front of the office.

"Did you get caught in a hang up on 61st at Broadway this morning?"

"Who us?"

They never answer.

CHAPTER THIRTY-NINE
Shadow and Fee Lo Do Not Testify

Jake is good to his word.

No assault ever happened at my office.

Badguy turned out to be just that. Jack McNelly was not his name, as we suspected. Those two venerated Texas Rangers can still rest in peace.

They brought McNelly's fall guy to the jail and were able to keep him twelve hours but did not to get him to talk. They locked him up in solitary in a holding cell and somehow, somebody still got something slipped into his oatmeal. He had it coming for sure since they pretty much established overwhelming cause to believe he smothered Sharon Rose Donaldson at her desk and rolled her out in a trash bag with the total lack of respect that both he and McNelly have for human life. And she was never shot at all with Ryan's police revolver. He finally got it back and avoided sanctions, and I suspected Jake's intervention; but we never asked how.

Fee Lo was off the hook for everything but the theft charge of intellectual property, which we both faced. I must admit that was a bell ringer. I had a new appreciation for someone facing felony charges and having to lawyer up as that term is used. I also had to consider the effect of having a possible indictment issued on a proposed charge by Rutter, which the majority of the people out there think is a responsible corporate entity. We told our story to the federal prosecutor.

Fee Lo had amazing information for Jake and the federal prosecutor that he gathered, literally under the cover of darkness as he got to know the East Field and what it was up to.

I don't think the federal DA believed a word we said. Granted it was pretty far-fetched but it was the best information anybody had gotten yet about what Rutter's run-away rebels were up to.

Flint had transferred Jake by then, because his real reason for being there was the on-going tracking of Ben Ramsey, whom I had known while Ramsey was passing himself off as an innocent young lawyer clerking for a State Appellate Justice and got caught up in a strange murder. Ramsey was an adept criminal who has evaded their capture for the entire time I have practiced law and that is apparently Jake's primary assignment. To follow Ramsey, but when he gets away, to put together the evidence to get those who hired him. The most surprising thing so far for me was that that little twerp Flint, stepped up and asked Rutter how much of the story they wanted out there and how they intended to provide reasonable assistance to the prosecutor, when the heavy side of the proof tipped the scales so deeply against them.

You never read a thing in the paper because the thing just went away. Rutter paid its fine, the largest ever assessed for a civil act. The government sealed the record. The formulas went into dark secrecy.

All Fee Lo and I were ever told was that the charges had been dismissed and the application by the complainant to expunge the record was granted. When a record is expunged, copies of the Order are filed with some fourteen public authorities that maintain such records and you are supposed to be free from any mention or reference for life.

In truth, I felt like bringing a civil suit to show what they had done and how close we came to international disaster when their chemicals and their water cleansing program got into the hands of terrorists. What we went through was emotional distress and the physical danger we were subjected to by their thugs. We were victims of false arrest since Rutter knew without any question that Fee Lo and I never stole their intellectual property; but had it dumped on us by a reporter that I was still not sure would not surface someday with the full story. We discussed it, Fee Lo and I, but decided that was a lot of additional stress only to get money from them and it wouldn't make the world better at all because they have so much money there is no amount that could be awarded in a single suit that would hurt Rutter Industries.

Fee Lo got an offer to come back to work in security, which he politely declined, and someone visited with Phyllis MacArthur, my kickass assistant, to see what kind of response we might make to an offer to do some work every now and then for Rutter ourselves. I wasn't there and the offer was never made to me, but I am very proud of Phyll for letting me know that she told them our docket was so full, it looks like we are going to have to add another lawyer to our staff already so it is unlikely that we can take on corporate defense work in any form.

We never found Dickerson—or even a hint that he had rescued Babe and that they were hiding out. In my heart I believe they are still alive. In my head I know that Ramsey is a cold-blooded killer, who would have taken them out because he had been paid to do so, had he ever found them.

After taking Fee Lo to the Crow's Nest to introduce him to Norma Sue, who is as sweet a Southern Girl as you would want to meet, he became so infatuated with her that it is keeping his thoughts off Babe for a while. He just looks at me when I ask how he's doing. That's a community up there around Bobby Gene and the Crow's nest in which I grew up that can fascinate you or disgust you. I'm somewhere in between since that's part of my family and I do love them. Bubba, the bodyguard and I grew up together around that old honky-tonk and among the movers and shakers there; we know some heroes and some fools and some are uncaring and selfish people. But when it's part of your family, you look at it differently. Fee Lo shakes his head a lot because he can't help but feel the energy around Norma Sue, and she's gaining fast in popularity and is already well known to local people, as he has discovered. She's a little crazy like us all, but she is the real thing and he seems to know it.

Phyll can take or not the fact Bubba is somewhat enamored with her. We have a strange relationship, Bubba and I, because we don't yet know if we are brother and sister, or cousins. His real name is Audy Murphy Jones and he is a permanent member of the entourage around General and the Crow's Nest. That's all he's ever known. No one's ever confessed to us the true nature of our bonds, but we are bonded and he is around when I need him; but he also has to take care of General because Millie won't do it anymore. She says she is through with General forever.

The old man is a story all by himself. Someday maybe we'll talk about that. Phyll says Bubba definitely does not have staying power and I believe that's probably true; but it is nice to see more of him, when he heads our way.

I can't help the fact that Phyll and I continue to look for Babe and

Dr. Dickerson. That singer did call me. Said what transpired between him and Babe was so tender, but, involving as it did breaking with Roger and destroying the group, he still can't deal with it yet.

I told him okay and to call me again when he felt like it and for us to keep talking about it. He explained to me that he is now a one-man orchestra and very popular, putting on private shows, doing weddings and he's even done some funeral parties. I won't believe it when I hear him, he tells me, but when he puts an act together, he is about five people with a fifteen-piece orchestra, all synthesized, and coming from one performer; but you can't tell it.

I wish him well and greater peace than he's had and hang up. I don't especially look forward to another call, since his talking time is two or three in the morning and that's about the time I get into my deepest rem sleep if I sleep.

The intellectual property accusation is no longer out there, but the documents Babe put in the deep well cooker at Fee Lo's apartment are still in my safety deposit box at Moody Bank and I guess they are safe from pilfering. For some reason Flint pulled back on his lawsuit to get them. Fee Lo made me promise to fight to keep them.

"I told Little Babe I would keep her and them safe," he says. "I let her down, but those damn papers are staying there."

I agreed because it makes him feel better.

Given Dr. Dickerson's note across a copy of the formula, the legal effect of those documents could be used as proof that one of the units at Rutter was producing an experimental substance, they said, to assist in the desalination of water in a new plant in the Middle East to meet its dire need for fresh water. Surrounded by salty water, the Middle East envisioned a major operation that Rutter provided the foundation for, using Dr. Dickerson's plans and intellectual property on converting salt water to pure. Rutter has already made boo-coos of big bucks on it.

But Fee Lo had managed to put himself into the center of what was going on out there and he took mental notes and played it back to Jake. The visiting scientist in the East wing, Lars Andersen, with the full support of that little old man at the top, who did nothing but walk the halls and tap his cane against the doors, convinced Jeremiah Rutter that the entire project had as its purpose spreading the one true faith across the Islamic world by a strange kind of war led by terrorists, that he was told were patriotic Christians. It was to be another Crusade using poisoned water to bring down anyone who considered Islam to be sacred. The formula that Dr. Dickerson tried to destroy was his colleague's combination of chemicals, which had strange effects on any living creatures in the desalinated water and had properties that had been outlawed for commercial generation since the old war games of mustard gas and other arsenic-based chemicals of the two World Wars. And they weren't headed for any legitimate business in the Emirates; they were marked for delivery to a roaming dessert tribe between Syria and Iran, which intended to sprinkle it in water sources throughout the area in order to take the territory.

That should not have been attractive to staid old Rutter Industries, a Texas standard in the business world; and Rutter proved to be pretty good at erecting a Chinese Wall—the name given to the federal statutes's requirement to section off the bad guys in a business; and it did so between that faction and the remainder of good old Rutter and establishing that none of the good guys knew anything about it. In fact, Rutter agreed to pay a fine of double the big bucks it had been paid before it failed to deliver.

Galveston did get another park out of the ill-gotten gain; I did bring that suit to set aside sufficient acreage for Sharon Rose Donaldson Park. Her Mother now thinks she died in a car accident doing work overseas for Rutter. Her house is paid for, her costs and expenses promised, and a public health nurse makes daily visits. When Phyll and I visit, she seems to be getting along, but she looks for her daughter every day because that is just what she does.

So all is well with the world.

Right?

Please tell me something good's gonna come out of this.

Babe, Fee Lo thinks, has not departed this life but is still out there somewhere putting together the expose that will bring her a Pulitzer; and I wish her well, frankly. But I don't think she ever gave a Tinker's damn for Fee Lo, or as it turns out, my cousin/bodyguard/investigator, Bubba, that she led down another primrose path to have him get her information. She used both, but gave Fee Lo a double dose at the end. Strange, isn't it? We can't help who we love, and that power of love is really incredible.

By the way, that water in the Coleman. Phyll and I should have gotten that clue a lot earlier and Fee Lo suffered a major disappointment that I had not read his clue immediately. The originals of the other PhD's formula for poison to take out villages in the Mid-East were stolen by Dickerson for Babe, who ended up somewhere with Dickerson, I'm convinced.

We flew to Marfa—Jake, Fee Lo, Phyll and me, and we found Goose and he swore, same as on a stack of Bibles, he said, that he hadn't seen the good Doctor or the little lady, whom he professed not to know at all. But I had those goods. My Buddy at the West Houston Airport sang like a trained canary. He described Babe to a T and let me know they'd flown out of there many times over the last couple of years.

So much for fealty to Fee Lo, but when it comes to taking someone's word, we all tend to trust that person who thinks the way we want them to think.

Fee Lo and Goose got along real well, and we covered that ranch almost foot by foot and it was locked up tighter than a drum. If anybody had been there in months, you couldn't tell. Goose even opened the cabin, which did have Babe's sense for spotlessness, which Phyll and I agreed on with just a nod. No other evidence suggested the presence of either of them. No toothbrushes on the cabinet, no razor in the drawer, no Listerine. I'm sure I saw the clearing that I was pretty sure he and Emmeline camped at, but I haven't talked to her in months now.

I think that won't be my last visit to that area. Roger Shutte knows Dickerson was working on that portable water desalinator and had been since his NASA days and Tilly would be happy to know, Yes, Dr. David did get the patent on it and Roger helped him get it. Babe sent him the painting by a local that was painted at Dickerson's ranch that does have a pump and a well, suggesting he has an active oil reserve and may not have to work in the future.

I only caught Shutte once looking at that painting but neither of us said anything.

If Babe is still walking, she is somewhere just like that where she can breathe free and make her come back plans. Of all the things in life, I'd bet on, the first one is that if she is still breathing, Babe Burnett will someday be awarded a Pulitzer.

. . .

"Mama says you don't start out by drowning the beans," Fee Lo says as he lights up his stove and starts to prepare supper for Phyll and me and this time, Norma Sue, who likes his loft. We are back to being a threesome, plus Norma Sue occasionally. Jake has gone on to greater things with the feds.

"Always remember that," he adds. "You cover them slightly so the water can do its work of softening them early. I sure had no time to come up with a new hiding spot and just knew you were already getting my message. Man was I acting fast."

"That big guy tried to push me through that window and I showed him. I went out the next one and circled the building until I got to the drain system and slid to the ground on it. He was so big he could not get through the window and by the time he got outside the wretched wreck and I were long gone. We are never gonna let anybody have that car," he says and I laugh.

Beneath the pot filled with water was what Rutter was looking for—the original for the formula for the desalination process, the chemicals used, marked out by Dr. David Dickerson's signature and the note, certifying that the mixture was "known to Rutter to be outlawed, deadly, and against all rules earthly and divine." The key phrase was known to Rutter to be outlawed. He used that specific language and he knew how much dynamite was added when he signed his name to it and dated it. Stored in a nice zip lock bag and tucked away by Fee Lo when they broke in and tried to kill him to get it. It lay there until Phyll and I found it. A single little slip of paper that would save the world if we could keep it from getting out.

And we did.

But it became one of those things locked away in the secret places never to be revealed.

Of course, Fee Lo was always protected by it. The villains couldn't make the mistake of killing him because he never gave an inch, hint, or waiver. As long as they had his Babe, they could not have broken him. They just messed up in the order they took them in.

Phyll fought off Harry/Chin until the late afternoon they walked into the back door of our office and found her somewhat in flagrante delecto with Audi Murphy Jones, whom she introduced to them as her fiancé. Harry/Chin had be consoled. Phyll, he says, is the first person he ever loved more than breaking concrete blocks. Rand knew she was putting on a show. He took off his investigator's white Stetson and put it on his chest over his heart and said quite royally: "Miss Phyll, this is not my first rodeo as you know; and I'm always gonna be around." Phyll is certain that neither of them has staying power. Not to her way of thinking anyway. If we could just bottle that power of love in the same container with Phyll's appeal and add maybe a dab or two of Fee Lo's testosterone, none of us would have to worry about going to work again.

Which is not the case for me.

The rent is due, Phyllis reminded me just this morning. She thinks the deposition of Hank the Hulk went well and Jay Lewis is beginning to ask about possible settlement. My credible witness is extremely credible since she was a teacher he laid into just a few short weeks before he assaulted my girl and took out her two front teeth, which is hard on a 16-year old prom queen. Lewis got cold feet when I said this kid really needs help and told Jay Lewis we wanted his parents to agree to that in any settlement: They would get him help. He shook his head. "This is a coach's kid," he says. "Sometimes it just ain't gonna happen. He's on varsity and A&M is looking at him."

So it might be a while before we settle.

And J. Edgar? Well, like the Badguy with two fake names any true Texan could spot a mile away, J. Edgar also wasn't who he said he was either. I should have known. J. Edgar is just too fake to be fooled by it. But what can I say? I guess I was just vulnerable. But those ten days he promised to use to convince me of anything with all that talk about, 'I finally found you and I'm not letting go', just didn't happen.

It was just talk or Flint saved him at the last minute and sent him out of town because when duty called, he was out the door.

He says he'll be back.

He also says, "I might not be where you want me to be every minute but as long as I hang on to this line of work, I gotta go when they call me to where they send me. But I'll be back and you won't find anybody better between now and then."

I say probably not, so that I can let him go.

But it was good while it lasted, I agree, and the big girls do say that's the test. The going up has to be worth the coming down; but it sure did go up and down real fast.

. . .

It hurt, Friend, but I don't want to talk about it yet. I've done a lot of thinking about it. Rationalizing.

I've told myself, it's okay to get played if you get something good out of it for yourself.

He did make me feel so special and my body fit with his perfectly. Everything he did to me, I was doing to him the same way with the same intensity and with the same feeling, so much so it was like making love to myself. I'll never be able to explain that anyway, so why try. I just put him in a file, deep in my brain. At least, one time in my life, I had the best. It would be a sin to think that is wrong or to regret something that good.

I got Fee Lo back into circulation so much, he actually took Norma Sue to meet his Mother, which he never did with Babe. He also took her in my wretched wreck rather than her chauffer driven limo and that sweet girl actually agreed to it. She gave me the choice of His Harley or her limo. Phyll chose the limo for us both. We parked the Harley and chained it.

That little bastard tested her and found out Norma Sue Calhoun distant cousin to the South Carolina Calhouns is the real thing. He promised his Mama he would never get on a motorcycle again, so he can't very well show up on the Harley. And Norma Sue had one ride on it; before she swore never to get on it again. That sweet girl even helped him put a serving of those beans into a Rubbermaid bowl so they could prove to his Mama her son could cook even if not just like her. They had so much fun doing that and I saw just how much Norma Sue is taken with my best friend.

As usual, I got stuck with the Harley because I couldn't see myself losing my good image by being dropped off at the Courthouse in a Limo. Phyll absolutely refuses to put her new-Lemon-Yello-tights-covered-derriere on that machine again ever; but, although I hate to admit this, I'm getting attached to it. I even like turning into the Government Building Parking Lot on 57th street every now and then and making a little noise because it still makes the deputies smile. All of them can't help but turn to see who's on it, me or Fee Lo, and every one of them waves me on without checking id as I walk by with my brief case slung over my shoulder. Makes my day the way heads turn.

I say to myself that I'm gonna get myself some of those soft kid leather boots instead of these I have to wear to hold up my bike.

I'm not sure they're as comfortable as people say; but I would do it for show. And I'm thinking about getting a Stetson, white, just like Jake's for the pure hell of it.

He looked kinda good in his; I think, so I should look mystifying. I would do it because I have an image with that bike and I have to maintain it. And all those government lawmen will nod and wave me though the gate because this is my hometown now. I am one of theirs!

I go straight to Edward Stevens' office when I get to the Courthouse.

"You have a minute?" I ask.

He pushes a file aside and sits back as I come into his office.

"Always," he says and smiles. "I heard Mother Fucker moved on."

I nod. "Business, I think," I say.

"I wondered how long it'd be before you showed up," he says. "Looking for a real man?"

"Is there one here?" I ask him seriously, but I know him well enough now to know this is his idea of a joke and I work hard to make sure he sees that it doesn't hurt.

"I don't want to mix business with pleasure. I want to talk to you about a case. But I'm also about to make you prove your bragging rights," I say and he knows I'm reading him and playing him at the same time. "You made me endure barbecue and your honky tonk, so I've decided to show you where I grew up on the wrong side of the tracks—that is Silas City, Texas—just Southeast of the big city."

"Do they have food?"

"Nothin' decent. A steak, which is not worth the money. But the music's good, people who drink beer like the home brew, and I like the way you move your body, Sir.'"

He laughs. "M'am you are the first person ever in my long life who said I could dance. I know I can dance, but somehow my partners in the past have all thought it's incumbent on a man not to step on their toes."

"Well that would be nice," I say. "I make no promises, one way or another," I say and he gets my message right off.

"I don't require any," he says.

"Good. That's decided. Now can you talk to me about this case? As long as you don't do something just for me, but still consider the issues, I think it's okay that I asked you out. I need to reciprocate, you know that."

"Oh, yes," he said. "That's the socially responsible thing for you to do. I took you out. You take me out."

And the rest is history, as they say.

He actually refused to settle my case, and I set it for trial by jury. He knows that on that case, I have the goods and will whip his ass when we get it to trial.

He just laughs.

When I send Roger Shutte another small contribution for the 401k Phyll and Fee Lo and I set up with him, I always ask if there's any word, because I figure if Babe is still breathing, she's stirring up trouble somewhere and hiding the goods with him as she did the Rutter papers not only to make them safe, I think, but to touch her home base, which I am convinced Roger still is.

Of course Little Babe is never totally out of mind for any of us.

Phyll and I see her Mama, Laverne, regularly and drop by to catch up with Jean Newman and Floyd Conner, the Coach, when he calls and says he has a brisket coming out of the oven at 1 p.m. on the dot. The last time, they met us together at his house for the third time and it seemed they might have been doing that a lot. But they and Mom say they've not heard from Babe. Mom says the cell phone's never rung and that it's only us she gets when she types in Babe.

We heard somebody bought her house, finally; and I was hoping Fee Lo would have one less place to drive by, just looking, but that proved not to be the case and somebody's locked it up and is not even paying the taxes but they are not foreclosing but are still keeping it locked up tight as a drum, as they say, so we have no way of knowing what's happening there. Oh well, life can always use a little mystery.

. . .

Friend, I'll try to tell you more when I have time; but tonight I have to think about how I'm going to try this next case I have coming up.

Another teen-aged boy, but considered an adult by the state, shot his best friend.

Right in the heart.

Both high on drugs.

He says he didn't mean to do it so they should let him go home and forget the charges. It was just manslaughter! He says.

That's what life seems to have come down to these days as if life is just another video game with these Millennials.

When you see her again, be sure to tell Clarice I made a point of telling you how much I love her!

You created a monster: Fee Lo now says I have to go see Bobby Gene and says he will go with me, but I can't do it again right now.

Love and Bye, Shadow.

CAROLYN MARKS JOHNSON has an eleven-book series about the Courthouses of Texas and the stories that flow from them. The series starts with these two, *Detention*, and *Rutter Industries*. Carolyn loves her work in the legal field but is an artist and writer. She was a reporter-photographer for newspapers in Austin, Dallas, Raleigh (NC) and Greensboro (NC). She won awards for investigative reporting.

A student of history, she held a Research Fellowship from the Lyndon Baines Johnson Library in Austin and studied in the Presidential Papers of Lyndon Baines Johnson, which provided the basis for her Master's thesis: "A Southern Response To Civil Rights, Lyndon Baines Johnson and Civil Rights Legislation l957-l960 (University of Houston, 1974). She holds a Master of Judicial Studies Degree from the University of Nevada's National Judicial College, writing, "Juror People Preferences, A Houston Jury Project."She taught History and Government at Alvin Community College (1974-81) and at the University of Houston as a teaching fellow (1972-74 and teaches 'Voir Dire and Jury Communication at South Texas College of Law (1998-Present). As an undergraduate at the University of Houston, Carolyn took Fourth Place in the *Atlantic Monthly's* nation-wide Literary Contest (1972); and the Louis Kestenberg Award for Outstanding Graduate Research Paper.

9 781622 882625